I0645230

**They were a small operation, up against a man who had wealth, power, and very *big* bodyguards...**

Wolf cleared his throat. "Just so you don't think I've been sitting around growing hair, Chico has my full report on that mazer theft two weeks ago. I think you'll find it interesting, Doc."

The Vax displayed a high angle shot of two men coming out of customs where they were greeted by a third man whom Pat recognized immediately. "Amos Brew," she said.

"Right," Wolf answered. "And the big guy in black is the one I tangled with after he shot Jonny. His full name is Crusher Cloud."

Pat watched the port-of-entry video carefully. This was the first time she seen the three-meter tall bruiser Wolf had told her about.

"That's Eric Von Roon," Wolf said, placing one of his information mods into the slot in the top of his head. "He's the CEO of Weave Corporation and he came here to meet with Brew, his local operations manager, to try and buyout Blue Star Industries. Crusher is registered as Von Roon's bodyguard."

St. Mathew whistled softly.

Tripleye ~ We never blink…

Early in the twenty-second century, a master of mind control has risen to the head of Earth's Weave Corp. Under the guise of the Neo-Socialists, he threatens to terrorize both the Inner and Outer Planets with murder, sabotage, and the theft of a strange bio-substance known as the Snot.

Against this malevolent foe, the mismatched ops of Tripleye use the LINK to mentally form an uneasy ensemble dedicated to fighting a madman's warrior elite. From the free-wheeling splendor of Vegas Space Station to the eerie ruins of an underground Martian city, the first private eye agency on Mars risks everything to stop the death-dealing powers of Weavc Corp.

# TRIPLEYE

## John Hegenberger

A Black Opal Books Publication

GENRE: SCIENCE FICTION/MYSTERY-DETECTIVE/FUTURISTIC

This is a work of fiction. Names, places, characters and incidents are either the product of the author's imagination or are used fictitiously, and any resemblance to any actual persons, living or dead, businesses, organizations, events or locales is entirely coincidental. All trademarks, service marks, registered trademarks, and registered service marks are the property of their respective owners and are used herein for identification purposes only. The publisher does not have any control over or assume any responsibility for author or third-party websites or their contents.

# DEDICATION

*To all the dream-makers out there.*

# CHAPTER 1

*CICATRIX*

*Mars, 2103*:

Some of the voices in Dan "Wolf" Archerson's head didn't bother him. The voices from the Link were okay, because limited telepathy was a normal part of working at Tripleye. And the voice of his mods was because selective memories were an essential part of every good investigation.

It was the broken, whispering voice from nowhere that haunted Wolf, which was why he was resting on Doc Pat's therapeutic couch.

From the pillow beneath his head, the relaxing endorphin complexes rose up to permeate—he wondered if that was the right word—the skin of his neck and finally his brain. Once in his system, the proteins would loosen his inhibitions and free him from the noise in his mind. Like the MediCen patch on his right ear, Wolf knew it was all for his own good. He belonged here. Lately he'd been screwing up too often. He felt confused and needed to understand why.

The doctor made a note of Wolf's neurological status and brought the lights down low. He thanked her dreamily, as she seemed to fade into the darkness. If anyone could help him, if anyone could assure him of an answer, he knew it was Doc Pat. He had worked with and for the woman for several years. She was the best therapist on the planet, and he wanted her help dealing with noise in his head.

For an instant, the sound seemed to come back. This time it was more like music—little riffs of intense rhythm, much faster than his normal sad blues. They had been mingling in his mind for the last ten days, along with the voice that called him by name. Then the couch's chemicals reached his cortex and slowly, gently, Wolf floated into soft, untroubled memory.

For therapeutic purposes, reality became replaced by the memories in Wolf's consciousness, and he slipped into "report" mode…

∽∾∽∾

*Breeep.*

My head was still aching from last night's binge. I

was right in the middle of shaving it, when the call came through on the Vax.

*Breeep.*

I pressed the copy key to shut the thing up and went back to spreading the depilatory around my brow and chin, careful not to get any near my eyes. The jazzblues wailed in my head, a cool sax quartet moaning out the classic "Harlem Nocturne." In the mirror, I watched the hissing foam burn through my three-day growth, the way a mazer melted permafrost.

The old man's mods taught me to live right—clean body, clean mind. To me, a clean body meant a scraped scalp and no more hair than a bar of soap.

Just as the quartet hit their last note, I finished drying, popped the mod out of my head, and gargled the last of last night's wine on my way across the room to read the Vax.

I had a premonition about the case the minute I viewed the message. Tracing stolen military weapons was always a ball buster. They wouldn't let you near the installation, or any of its people. So how were you supposed to find out anything?

Wiping my face and shrugging into a clean jacket, I keyed a call to Lieutenant Commander Garvis, who'd handed the case to Tripleye. He explained that the government already had conducted a thorough investigation of the missing mazer guns over the last three months. Then he admitted they had come up with nothing. That meant the trail was three goddamn months cold, and the weapons now could be anywhere on Mars, or even off planet. He'd sure appreciate it if we could look into the matter. There was a ten percent bounty.

Ten percent wasn't jackshaft! I was pissed and insulted, so I decided to link to Chico rather than use the Vax.

'*What's the deal, here?*' I asked her. '*I'm going to have to walk all over town on this assignment. Has the Doc gone nuts, or is the Agency just desperate for clients?*'

Chico linked back in her husky voice that she knew I lusted after. '*Take it easy, Wolf. Tripleye isn't listed in the outstanding receivable reports—yet. And Doc's just fine, thanks.*'

'*Then why are we taking on this low-return bounty?*' I said, feeling the first effects of the stiffness sawing into my nerves. I didn't mind using the Link, but I hated being held fixed stiff by its side-effect.

'*Look, tough guy, quit complaining,*' she replied. '*Use your mods to reference crooks and scuzz-bars. That'll save a lot of legwork.*'

With deep concentration, I answered, '*I'm not complaining. I'd take field work any day over a dull desk job like yours, but this is the kind of assignment that makes me seriously consider putting in for coldsleep.*'

She laughed, and I wondered again how she could stand the Link's irritation. Of course, she could stand me, so I guess that meant she could stand just about anything. *'Well, you're not alone,'* she said. *'The doctor is sending over a backup op for you to take along. He needs the experience.'*

*'Oh, god! Not that kid? Jesus.'*

*'Hey, Wolfy, you're a tough guy.'*

*'Yeah, but—'*

*'You can take it. Bye.'*

I came out of the Link wanting to punch through a wall of woven carbon, or to kick something all the way to Deimos. Damn baby-sitting, that's what it was. I was expected to teach this new kid how to do my job. Pretty soon, the agency wouldn't even need me for that!

Why didn't Doc just use mods for instruction? Mods could teach you more than any human instructor, but people were afraid to have the operation on their brains. Stupid, base fear. And they could learn so much so easily, too. Shit!

There was a knock at my front door. When I opened it I found the long-haired kid humming and tapping a tune on his pants legs with a pair of McCoke chop sticks.

"Hi, partner." He smiled. "I'm Jonny Jesus. Tripleye sent me over to be your backup."

I wanted to coldcock him. I took a deep breath and jerked my thumb for him to come inside. "Everybody calls me Wolf," I told him. "You screw up and I'll chew your ass."

The kid nodded as he came in and looked around. I

didn't say anything else to him, while I finished getting dressed. He sat beside the Vax and hummed quietly to himself. Confident little jerk.

There was really nothing to using a mod. A lot of people had them fifty years ago. But the kid had never seen on up close before, so I had to endure his eager interest.

"What did it feel like to have the operation?" he asked.

I shrugged while rummaging through the assortment of programs, looking for the one my father had labeled, "Squealers."

Stored memories were a necessity in a small and growing town like Achilles. But they were also a hindrance, because they were full of random and amateurishly inscribed info, kind of like the way the internet used to be before it crashed during the war. Still, if you wanted to access volumes of data while out on a case, or needed special training in a hurry, memory modules could save you hours—sometimes years—of reference and education. "It was done when I was born," I lied. "My old man was part of the Settlers sect and believed in passing on as much info as possible, directly and early—just to be safe."

"Yeah? I'm a Samaritan, so I don't know who my dad was yet. But the Clan just about split with pride when I quick-colonized to Mars." He laughed. "See, if I do well here, I get to—"

"That's great, kid," I said. "Now keep the noise dampened, will you? I'm scanning."

He watched in fascination when I lifted the tissue flap and slid the mod into my fontanel, where it fit into place between the hemispheres of my brain. The program made contact, and I felt the familiar warmth spread over me as the data dropped into my system. I knew, suddenly, all the filed information within the mod. It was a little like walking up hill against the wind, but you couldn't beat the psychosomatic thrill of info rushing past you almost faster than you could comprehend. Then the warmness faded and you could deal with the data flood and sort through the details.

George Davis, illegal substances: Wilber T2, blue collar crime; Shan Conner, white collar; Steve Canyon III, shakedowns and blackmails; Dr. Bill "The Pill" Houston, illegal operations; Hugh Meek, freelance muscle; Bunny Tax, syntha-sex; Skye Williams, counterfeit explosives and armaments—That was the one: Skye Williams!

She checked out in detail as a Mar/Cau, thirty-seven, B, B, 58cm with an arrest record that went back twenty-five years to 2078. She was a drifter, never showing a legal income. Since the info in the mods was several years old, I was taking a chance on scanning for known associates and frequented locations, but I decided it was a hell of a lot better than asking conspicuous questions on the street.

The kid was singing along with some commercial on the Vax when I popped mod out and slid it back into a pouch in my belt. "Okay, Jesus," I called, reaching for my hat. "I've gotta to go out. You stay here, until I—"

"Whoa, partner," he interrupted, "Doc said where you I go."

"I know what she said, but I'm calling the shots now, so—"

"I can't learn anything sitting in your apartment, Mr. Wolf. Come on. Let's get into some field work."

He jumped up, shut off the Vax with a smack of his palm, and went humming into the corridor with all the sass and confidence of youth. Sure, I envied him, because he was right. The one thing a mod couldn't teach you was how to deal with people in the real world.

We hired a couple of cycles at the intersection of Third and Lincoln and pedaled our way through the tunnels. The Lithium mines were between shifts, so the traffic was light enough that he could ride his cycle alongside me. Lucky me.

"So, what's the Link feel like?" he asked.

I shifted gears to get more traction as we approached the Spiral near Main Street. Tripleye didn't administer the Link to an operative until after the first six months. It was a shakeout period, while background details were checked and a medical and psycho history could be fleshed out by Doc Pat. The kid was anxious to get on line and experience the numbing sensation of limited telepathy. I could tell he'd be in big trouble with the other ops, if he continued his habit of singing under his breath.

"It's a bit like falling asleep." I steered to the right. "Only you get to pick up on someone else's dreams and you can talk to them about it." *That ought to confuse him.*

"Sounds great! So why does the gov ban it? Is it addictive?"

"No," I said slowly "But you know how the gov operates. They're not happy in the CapDome unless they control the whole planet. Ask them to do any real work, though, and they quickly find an excuse to debate or subcontract it."

"What do you mean?"

We coasted together around a corner.

I'd already said too much, but dammit I felt the urge to pitch a bitch today about any topic that came my way. I was supposed to be teaching this kid his job, right? So I might as well tell him which side his bread was frozen on.

"Who do you think hired us for this job?"

"Not the gov," he said. "I heard it was some lieutenant commander in the military."

"Same thing," I wheezed, realizing I'd been pedaling much faster than necessary. I brought the cycle to a stop and the kid did, too.

"Look," I said. "Tripleye's got a contract with the gov to test the Link. We're the experimental betas, get it? So far, the majority of folks can't take the stuff. It passes through their bodies like excess vitamins. But one person out of every two or three hundred has some sort of allergy. They go into a coma and don't come out, so Doc's working on a cure or solution or counter-agent or something.

"But the gov's not about to permit another epidemic like the GRGA virus. So until it's satisfied with our long-term results—which probably means after we're dead—it won't let anyone else use the Link. In the meantime, we go about our business, doing grunt surveillance, data checks, and high-risk, low-grade investigations, like this one, which the military has already screwed up. Get it?"

A double-decker wagon rattled past, delivering lunch to the miners. I knew I was lecturing, but that was part of the assignment. If the kid was smart, he'd keep his mouth shut and maybe learn something.

But he wasn't smart. He was suspicious. "How come you know so much about Tripleye operations?"

I pushed off on the cycle and called back over my shoulder. "Because, I used to own it."

"Replitropic!" he said, as we rode through the Main Mall. "You used to own the agency?"

"Yep. My father started it in the early '80s. Intensive Investigations, Incorporated, was the first independent detective business on Mars. That was during the big relocation allowance from Earth. We mostly did credit checks, debuggings, and process servings, but it was a profit from the first year."

He listened as we coasted past Christopher Village, where a group of schoolkids were lined up to go inside and learn about Achillian history. *I guess that's why I keep jawing about my own experiences.*

"I joined right after graduation, when I was seventeen. Worked at it ever since. Sixth-generation private eye, thanks to the skills and knowledge in my father's mods."

We neared our destination. "So why'd you sellout?"

"I didn't sellout," I answered. "I was bought out. It was a good deal, too. Come on. This should be the place we're looking for."

Up Yours was an early popular eating and meeting place, originally built by Charlie Brew, before he got heavily into debt from Quark Racing. In the late '60s, lots of food and old Earth charm used to spread from the place all up and down Byte Street.

But that was over forty years ago, and nothing in Achilles changed more quickly and more permanently than the popularity of party spots. Today, Up Yours was a dark and battered habitat for fuzzheads, lazy or politically-dissatisfied workers, and top-level executives on their way down the ladder. Some of this I knew from experience with other bars in the area, and some of it came from the "Location" mod I'd slipped into my head right before walking through the front entrance.

The kid followed, whistling casually.

I had zeroed in on Up Yours because Skye Williams

used to hang out here. I had a rough idea what "hang out" meant, but it didn't look like anybody had dangled much of anything in this dump for some time.

*So, this is what an Earth saloon looks* like, I thought. *Lots of gaudy signs promoting mildly-addictive substances and flashy mini-holos that advertise for patriotism and sex.* High on a shelf behind the counter, a Vax played nothing but static. Two pale-skinned guys in the back played some sort of gambling game based on the number of rebounds achieved with a little yellow ball. A long-haired girl sat in the corner by the entrance, doing sand art. She was too young to be a forty-year-old explosives dealer.

I targeted two men tossing dice at a table near the counter as my best source of info and headed in their direction. The barkeep, a broad, balding man with one arm, looked up from the dice as the kid and I approached.

"Nice hat," he said cautiously. "Uh, Indian head-dress?"

"Twentieth-century fedora," I answered. "Chicago."

"Oh, yeah. Never seen one close up before. Looks real good on you." He turned to the bar. "Get you something?"

The kid leaned in on the dice game like he wanted to play, but the two rollers ignored him. I thought about having something, just to work out the kinks in my back, but I shook my head no and asked the guy running the place if he could put us on to Skye Williams.

The expression on his face told me I'd just shit in the bakery.

"We don't want no trouble," he said, pushing at me with his one arm. "You understand?" The dicers started to get out of their chairs, and Jonny backed away from the table.

"Hey, I hate trouble," I said quickly. "Nobody here's got nothing to worry about."

"We're just looking for a little information," the kid said to the room at large. There was that sass and confidence again, only this time, I didn't envy it.

"And, we're more than happy to pay for it," I added.

The girl playing in the sand slipped quietly out the front door behind us, as the two pale guys in the back stopped their game and watched the show.

"Skye ain't been in here for years," the barkeeper said.

I looked at the others to see if they were going to agree. They looked back at me to see if I was going to buy it.

I started to explain again, but the kid took a more direct approach. He picked up a chair and slammed it on the floor in front of the crowd of glaring men. "What do you know about stolen gov mazers?" he asked one of the dicers, and I felt my skin tighten.

The man stared back at the kid and spat on the floor. I figured he wasn't one of the top-level executives on the way down.

"What do you know about my dork?" the man said.

Cautiously, I fingered the pouch in my belt where I kept the "Hand-to-Hand" mod. I was considering using it on the kid.

The barkeeper tried to defuse the situation by asking us to leave.

"Two hundred credits," I said. "That's what we'll pay for a lead to Williams. Any takers?"

"Forget it, partner," the kid said, and I felt an adrenaline rush at his next words. "This guy's going to tell us for free."

I had time to and take one step back before the kid grabbed the dicer, and the other three men jumped all over us. The bar keeper howled and ran for the counter, while somebody pulled a club and began swinging it in my direction.

I cursed and brought an arm up in time to block the blow. The guy who was hitting me was one of the ball bouncers and his arm was as thick as my thigh. He grimaced at me with two even rows of cheap, plastic teeth set in an unshaven jaw covered with black and white whiskers.

I hate hair, so I hit him with both fists in the face. He fell back, and I was going to turn and see how the kid was doing when someone else rammed me in the back and sent me sprawling forward into the dice table.

I got kicked twice before I could roll under the table and get back on my feet. I came up in time to catch the kid flying ass over elbows on top of me, a tangled weight that drove the breath out of my chest. Somebody threw a chair on us, but I was too busy working my lungs to care about it. I got kicked again and cursed the kid for his stupid brashness. Then something rock hard and yellow bounced off the right side of my skull and I broke through a wall to blurred, hot slumber.

It lasted maybe five seconds. Then the mod's standard stimulus program ripped the top of my head off and flushed my brain with what felt like a bucket of electric blood.

My eyes popped wide with berserker fury, every muscle jolted by the sudden bio-electric feedback. For a second, I couldn't speak, couldn't think, then I saw the bearded guy I'd slugged with both fists running out the door with my mod belt dangling from his fist.

I got up, grabbed the kid by his hair with one hand and my hat with the other, and rushed for the door. The dicer was pedaling like mad on one of our cycles.

"Come on," I told the kid. "There's our lead."

We took off after the guy, running to the nearest intersection. I clutched my Fedora and the kid held a sleeve to his bloody nose. We found two cycles parked at a residential area. Our man was almost out of sight, when we spotted him turning down the east corridor in the direction of the Ruins. *Shit*, I thought, *if he gets in there, we'll probably lose him.*

I used the "Location" mod, still in my head, to estimate his chances of escape, and then I pulled to a stop on the outskirts of the vast storage cavern and linked an update to Chico.

The kid could apparently tell I was linking. "Well? Do we go in, or wait, or what?"

"If I followed your style, we'd rush right in and get our heads smashed." I started scanning through the mod for info on the Ruins, so I didn't hear his reply.

The Ruins were a jumble of more than six hundred cliff-side rooms, open to each other like a maze built into one wall of the cavern room and illuminated by piezos-and. They were over six thousand years old and nobody knew who built them. Or, rather, we knew the original Achillians built them, but we didn't know what happened to the Achillians. The estimate was that these primitive people had lived off bread molds and fungus fibers, which had dried up when the water vented out to the surface from a series of marsquakes. Of course, that was all theory, but my father had filed it in the mod, and I was forced to listen to it, if I wanted the full story on the Ruins.

Over the last ten years, the city had taken to using the cavern as a warehouse for non-perishable supplies and stockpiled emergency goods. Thus, there were rows and rows palletized crates, packages and discarded dome construction materials piled high and generally forgotten. And, somewhere down there was the fuzzhead with my mods.

The kid was almost screaming at me. "What do we *do*?"

I looked at the high complex of sandrooms and aisles of containerized materials. "We don't have any choice. We go in."

He spun around. "I love it!"

The rest of the day, we tried to find the guy with my mods. This was the kind of investigation work with which the gov and the security police never would have bothered. It was what had made Intensive Investigations, Inc. a success. My father had never shirked from hard work, and neither would I. "Nothing to it, but to do it," he used to say. "Pick 'em up and put 'em down."

My old man was one hell of a detective. He knew every slogan in the book.

The kid hissed at me. "I found them," he whispered, as I joined him on something like the eighth level of the old Achillian complex, where we could hear muffled voices.

"Must be a couple of levels under us," I said to the kid.

"Or over us. I think they're this way."

We moved carefully through the rooms, expecting to encounter a lookout, but there didn't seem to be any guards, and pretty soon we were looking down on a room illuminated by broken and crumbling panels of piezos-and, where three men were in a heated argument. One was my buddy from Up Yours. He was doing most of the talking and it sounded like he had a lot at stake. Another guy wore a dark security guard outfit, so he was probably the warehouse watchman.

The third guy was one of the biggest men I'd ever seen. His face was broad, blunt, and wooden, his nose as flat as if it had been punched by an impact welder. His forehead was a wide blank surface perfectly perpendicular to the line of sight from his dull, unblinking eyes. His whole body was wrapped in a black, loose-fitting suit that hooded his head tightly around the outer edge of his face. His black gloves and soft shoes fit snuggly over his hands and feet.

The big guy was assembling something at a workbench and listening to the fuzzhead squeal about our scramble in the bar.

"So, you've got to take me with you, Crusher," the bearded guy was saying. "I've done like you told me and proven I believe in the Cause."

The big guy in black tightened down a cartridge and slotted in a packet on the side of what I now recognized to be a modified mazer gun.

The security guard stepped forward. "Only the elite can be part of our final operation. You've been paid well, and that's the end of it."

"No," our boy cried in earnest. "You promised you'd take me with you. Where's Skye? She'll stand up for me. I want to talk to Skye."

As if on cue, the security guard slammed the squealer against a wall and the big guy turned and fired the mazer, bathing my buddy in a white, translucent field of light that evenly constricted to half its original diameter in less than five seconds. The big guy, Crusher, had modified the mazer into a splat-light, like the ones they used in the Belt to temporarily hold prisoners. But there was something different about this one. When the big guy shut the weapon off, the shrinking didn't end.

Somehow it continued to pin the howling man within the tightening field of now-opaque light, bunching him up into a screaming ball and still pressing farther, like a self-containing tractor beam. The man cried out in pain as the pressure increased, shifting tighter from white to pink to red.

The screams became muffled. The ball settled on the floor and began to let off steam, shrinking to less than the size of my hat. Hissing now, the red color darkened to black and the tiny ball and its gruesome contents became no larger than my fist. I looked at the kid, who was held in rapture by the sight taking place below us.

When I glanced back, the ball was a black dot that completely shriveled out of existence, and Crusher laughed with a deep, base roar.

The kid and I backed away from the hole in the roof. I had seen some pretty incredible crap in my time, but this topped them all. I swallowed dryly. "Jesus."

"What?" the kid answered, more shaken than I.

I looked at his sweating, questioning face and realized I had just said his name.

"Replitropic!" the kid whispered. "I can't believe it!" His voice cracked with anxiety. "They just—You saw—"

I shushed him and linked to Chico. *'You've got to get us some backup. We've just witnessed one hell of a homicide.'*

*'Stay put,'* she said. *'I'll notify security.'*

*'No, no! There's a cop here already! He was in on the killing. Some fuzzhead we followed from the bar just got squeezed to death by a modified splat-light. This place is like a weapons chop-shop. Get some backup, but not the cops!'*

*'Hold on. I'll tell Doc.'*

The kid was humming a tune to himself, quietly. It was a fast tempo thing that pretty well indicated the level of his nervousness. "What'd they say?"

"Just hang easy," I cautioned him with the wave of a hand. What a time to be baby-sitting.

*'Wolf?'*

*'Yeah?'*

*'Doc says sit tight and watch for a chance to snatch the weapons.'*

*'Shit, princess, there's a 255 cm, 200kg guy here dressed in a black bodysuit and a flat face. His name's Crusher and it's no joke. See what you can find out about him, will you?'*

*'Can't you just check your mods?'* she asked.

*'No, godammit. They took 'em.'*

*'What?'*

*'Never mind. Just check.'* The Link's stiffness was beginning to make my back ache.

*'Take it easy, tough guy. We'll get St. Mathew there as soon as we find him. He's off the Link again. In the meantime, keep your temper down and send Jonny Jesus home.'*

*'Right. But when I get back, Doc and I are going to have a little chat.'*

*'It's always a pleasure hearing your insights, Wolfy.'*

I briefed the kid on our situation and he gave me nothing but flack. What I hated most about him was that the young jerkhead thought he already knew everything important about the investigating business. Hell, I'd seen better op candidates come back fragged from the Belt Wars. Well, a few more months of working at Tripleye would melt his positive spirit down to a sound and reasonable attitude, like mine.

"No way," he said, combing his long, shaggy hair. "You might be here all day. I can't leave you alone."

"Then at least get us something to eat," I said. "We passed a McCoke on the way here." I figured I'd try anything to get rid of him. Maybe he'd get cold feet and run.

"Okay. How about some pecopaste and VO?"

"Ugh! How can you eat that stuff?"

He cocked his head to one side. "I'll bet breadmeats and wine are to your taste. Right?"

"Wine is fine," I sighed. "Just keep your ass under cover."

He saluted and slipped around the corner.

I linked back to Chico.

'*Did you tell Doc I was on a homicide with an inexperienced jerkhead for a backup? Where the hell's St Mathew? Get that lieutenant commander on the Vax and tell him we've found his missing mazers.*'

'*Easy. Wolf,*' she said. '*You don't want to have a seizure, lover. Doc's working on a backup for you from the gov. Is the kid coming in, or not?*'

'*I don't think so.*' I grimaced. '*He went for pecopaste and VO.*'

'*That takes guts.*'

I broke the Link and eased forward to sneak another peek at the activity below. The security cop was gone. Two new men came in carrying small packages of electronic parts, which they took to the workbench where the big guy was building more weapons. I decided the light-constricting ball was some kind of combination splat-light and tractor beam, which meant off-planet R and D. We had the piezo-tech to balance the gravity and light throughout the city, but only one of the big, Earth-based corporations would be smart enough to bridge the technologies to create a weapon that did what I had witnessed.

Chico linked back. '*Wolf, we've got a few problems here. The military say they'll void the contract, if they have to come in and get the mazers. Do you want to pull out?'*

*'Not if it means we don't get paid.'*

*'Okay. We're still working on getting you some help. I'll come out myself, if I have to.'*

*'No, princess. You stay there. It's just surveillance duty, now. The danger's past.'*

*'You can't lie to me, Wolf Archerson. You're on the Link, remember?'*

*'All right, so it bothers me. Stay off my back, okay?'*

She was quiet for a moment. *'I haven't been able to locate anything about your big guy in black. And Doc says that if the kid comes back, you're to hang onto him.'*

*'Jesus shit, Chico! I'm not running a goddamn shiftschool! He could get hurt out here!'*

*'I thought you said it was just surveillance work.'*

*'It is, but he's driving me nuts, always fidgeting and picking at things.'*

*'You know, sometimes, you're sort of a baby, yourself, Wolfy. Jonny's got to learn what this job is really like. Stay close to him and he'll do fine. You were young once, too, so give him a chance.'*

I felt the painful stiffness creeping into my joints. *'I'd like to kick his comb up his ass,'* I said. The Link was a killer today.

To my surprise and further annoyance, the kid came back, but he had my favorite brand of wine with him, so we ate and drank and waited together for the next half hour.

I'd found another room that gave us a view of the entrance to the "weapons lab," plus easier access to the main route in and out of the Ruins. It seemed like the best place to stay, if we were in for a long wait. We planned to drop down into the lab and get the mazers, if the thieves left. Then, when St. Mathew showed up, I figured he could help us carry them all back to the nearest public intersection. In the meantime, I listened to the kid analyze me, which wasn't much better than his choice of music.

"You're a very violent man," he said. "You've never had any qualms about it until lately. Now, your biggest problem is that you haven't changed enough. It's as if you've been half-formed—"

"Will you cut the crap?" I said. "Or I'll yank your goddamn hair out! In this business, you've got to be tough, or they'll eat you alive. If that upsets you, take a pill."

"I'll bet your father was bald," he said, and it took all of my will power to keep from punching his lights out.

This and a lot more nonsense came out of him while he tapped his fingers on his knees and gave me a brief history of his short, little life.

He swore his name really was Jonny Jesus. He'd been born in the USA and shipped out to Mars as a vanguard for his religious group. They expected to make a lot of money in the field of inter-system corporate investigations. I had to laugh. He felt that there were "significant and fascinating religious possibilities" between the Link and common prayer. I laughed again.

"If I do well," he said in dead seriousness, "I'll get to have a full family and they'll tell me who my father was, so I'll be connected to my heritage. It's very important for a Samaritan to know his heritage and to be somebody."

"Jesus," I said again.

"By the way," he said without a pause, "what's your real name? Wolf sounds phony to me."

I thought about what Chico said. The kid wasn't intentionally obnoxious. He just acted that way. And he had been brave enough and considerate enough to come back with my wine, when he could have ducked out. Over all, I had to give him high marks as a quick thinker and his irritating aggressiveness might only be an aspect of his eagerness to learn and gain his heritage. Ha!

I rolled all the food containers into a ball and buried them under the sand.

"What the hell," I said. "It can't hurt. My name's Dan. Dan Archerson, but don't spread it around. Everybody else calls me Wolf."

"And you like it," he said in a calm sort of voice. "Thanks, Dan. You can trust me to keep your secret."

That got to me for some reason, but before I could answer, the warehouse security cop and two other guys scrambled into the room like an assault team and told us at gunpoint to shut up and lie flat. The acid in my stomach started to boil.

Naturally, I updated Chico as fast as thought. She said St. Mathew had linked to her and she had passed our location to him. He was on his way, but he wouldn't say what he had in mind for helping us.

Jules St. Mathew never said what he had in mind. He was a loner and he hated using the Link. If Doc hadn't gotten him off those embezzlement charges when he'd tested positive, St. Mathew would still be under armed guard, working the sandpits. The guy had an ego problem that would reach from here to Phobos. By comparison, his convictions about teamwork and comradery made me look like an entertainment director on a sexcursion cruise.

The two guys with the security cop turned out to be dockrats employed at the public accelerators. They led us down to the lab we'd been watching and, after a quick frisk, trussed us up with shipping bands.

I got my first close-up look at Crusher and relayed it to Chico, while my arms slowly grew numb from their bindings. I'd held up to electro torture before, but this guy didn't go in for the fancy stuff, he just pounded at us with his fists.

"Who sent you here?" the big man thundered only centimeters from my face. His eyes were clear as plex, his skin was grey and lifeless. I had never seen anyone so…two-dimensional. He reminded me of those wireheads on Vegas. There was something missing in him.

Even with the force of his insistence, I got the impression that he was running on remote.

"We got lost shopping," I told him. "Any of you guys know the way back to the Mall?"

Crusher slammed a massive fist into the side of my head, knocking me against the workbench where, through blurred vision, I could see my mods and belt lying next to a jumble of mazer parts. My hat lay in the dirt on the floor.

The kid was smart. He kept his mouth shut and was unconscious in less than a minute, but the cop was interested in the mod port in the top of my head. Through my pain, I heard him say something about hostages, and the Crusher's deep voice responded with the word "terminal." I felt myself hefted by the big guy and saw two of the dockrats carry the kid, while the cop shoved my mods and the other stuff in a large bag. We all piled into a security van and headed up the spiral to the Domes.

*'Where the HELL is St. Mathew?'* I linked. *'We're moving to the surface. I think these guys are taking the mazers off planet!'*

*'I'm trying to get him, Wolf,'* she said. *'Doc is going—'*

*'Trying?'* I screamed in my mind. *'Tell Doc we're going to be sucking vacuum if that son-of-a-tube doesn't get here in five minutes!'*

*'Doc's on her way to the surface and I'm calling security now.'*

I came out of the stiffness just as we were leveling off to the plain of Achilles's upper surface. Through the wide, tinted plex of the van's opposite window, I could see the rows of shipyards, smaller domes and storage tanks that ran along the roadbed connecting the landing pads with the accelerator terminals. A gang of plumbers were busy finishing the waterline expansion from the northern tundra station. They worked in pres-and-temp suits, outside the dome, only a few meters from where the van stopped and Crusher unloaded us, but they might as well have been on Neptune for all the good it did me and the kid.

Inside the small office of one of the many private shipping terminals, I was thrown into a chair and finally introduced to Skye Williams. She was the woman who'd been playing with the sand in Up Yours.

"You sure don't look forty," I said, admiring the smoothness of her skin and the shape of her figure.

"I spent five years in a prison gang and had to learn a trade to get out," she told me. "Cosmetology."

I couldn't help barking a laugh. Once again, the info in my mods was out of date. In another year or two, they would be of very little use to me. And a whole lot sooner than that, if I didn't get out of here.

"Hurry it up," she instructed the dockrats, handing Crusher a black, two-gallon pressure canister and putting the bag in a storage locker. "The ship is almost loaded and I've arranged a priority launch on number three public accelerator in ten minutes."

'*St. Mathew,*' I linked. '*Where the HELL are you?*'

Crusher looked at me with his cool, transparent eyes. "As soon as we're off," he told the dark-haired woman, as he left to board the shuttle, "kill them."

'*Chico? Doc? Anybody!*'

'*Just stay calm, skinhead,*' St. Mathew answered. '*I'm coming in now.*'

There was a knock at the door.

At first, I didn't recognize him. He had on one of his goddamn disguises—an elder in full vestments, with his long, blond hair pulled back and tied tightly in a tail.

"Oh dear me," he said, when the Williams woman answered the door. "I must have the wrong terminal." Then he froze and linked to me, '*Distract the bitch.*'

With a little hesitation, I tilted my chair over and crashed to the floor with a grunt. My right arm was completely numb, but the kid was coming back to consciousness.

St. Mathew didn't hesitate at all. His swift, upward-flowing kick caught the woman in the chin and snapped her head back. She fell to the floor with a thump, as St Mathew gracefully landed ready for further action in a modified mantis crouch.

The kid mumbled, "Is he praying, or what?"

"There are at least three more and a big guy in black out back. Get us out of these bindings!"

St. Mathew smiled and cocked his head. "You look nice like that. Perhaps I should let them ship you to Ceres."

I started to see red, but he pulled a butterfly knife from his sleeve, flipped it artfully, and cut us loose.

'*Chico,*' I linked, '*why didn't you tell me St. Mathew was coming in like that? I thought you and I were—*'

'*Sorry, Wolf. I've been busy working with Doc. She's trying to get the launch cancelled. The cops should be there in a few minutes. I've already called MediCen for a stretcher. What else did you want?*'

St. Mathew responded before I could. '*Chico, old girl, I love you, but I'm sure that we can take care of these boys all on our own.*'

'*The hell we can!*' I said, working the numbness out of my arm. '*Send security cops. And lots of them!*'

The kid looked at St. Mathew. "Where'd you learn that fancy kick?"

St. Mathew put a hand on Jonny's shoulder and I knew what was coming next. "The High Lama of Olympus Mons, son."

I kicked the locker open and dug into the bag stuffed there, hoping to collect my mods. "I know they put them here," I growled, dumping the bag's contents in a pile on the floor.

The kid and St. Mathew waited at the rear door, while I continued to retrieve the last contacts with my father. I had to make sure I had them all.

"Will you hurry up, Wolf?" St. Mathew asked, the calmness going out of his voice.

I snapped on the belt and pocketed the mods. "Okay. Let's burst this place."

St. Mathew looked at the kid. "I think he means he's ready to leave now, but with Wolf, you never know for sure."

"Hey," the kid replied, "I guess I know what he means. He's my partner, isn't he?"

St. Mathew and I looked at each other in mild surprise. The kid was holding up pretty well, considering. I decided to take a chance, figuring the situation warranted us all being in full contact.

"Here," I said, handing Jonny one of my back-up squibs. "Inject this like I show you, and you'll be on the Link for about ten minutes."

He smiled and eagerly administered the drug to the muscles in the back of his neck.

"Come on," I told them, knocking the door open with my shoulder. "Follow me." And that's when I caught the blast on the right side of my head.

It burned like fire. My muscles automatically threw me to the left as the kid came out and took a direct hit, cutting him from armpit to liver and tossing his body into St. Mathew's arms.

I was stunned not only by the glancing mazer blast, but by the sight of Jonny's death. He had been my responsibility. He'd been following me!

Rage erupted from a tiny dot in my brain to a killer haze that filled my body. '*Don't die, kid,*' I linked, while struggling back to my feet and into the aisle way. The next few seconds weren't very clear. St. Mathew must have gotten the kid to the Stretcher—I didn't know. Chico linked to me, but I didn't answer. I was running on my own internal drive and didn't hear her. She says I got up and beat the shit out of the other two dockrats, while the Crusher guy climbed aboard a mini-shuttle.

How I got on board the ship was a complete blank. The next thing I recalled fully was being attacked by an array of sharp-edged weapons. Some of them were like the knives used in freefall combat, only more…ancient. One had a hatchet-like head, others were shaped like tantos and stilettos, flashing, hissing and slicing at me under the dexterous control of the Crusher, all with deadly intent. I had no clear idea what to do, but my mods gave me the skill to tell my body when to dodge, weave, and kick in a flurry of blows, as the mini-shuttle slowly tracked along its path to the accelerator.

I saw that Crusher guarded the black canister Skye had given him, over everything else. I wanted to link to St. Mathew, or Chico, but I couldn't afford to have my body become stiff or out of control for a single second. Crusher came at me again, and I kicked him with all my strength, knocking the black canister from its mooring.

The attack stopped, gaining me precious seconds, while the giant in black tried to initiate the launch and lock the canister back into place at the same time.

Again I got the impression that Crusher wasn't his own man—hat he was under someone else's control, because a normal guy wouldn't have stopped his attack. He would have…well, crushed me.

The hatch had become partly unsealed during our fight and I wedged it open with the broken lid from one of the splat-light cases. I realized that our battle had forced Crusher to give up his plans to launch from the public accelerator. He was going to gamble that the thrusters alone would be strong enough to escape the planet's gravity well.

That was enough for me. I snatched up one of the splat-lights and, fumbling to prime and load it, fired blindly into the cabin, while rolling out the hatch into the airless cold. My lungs immediately slammed shut.

*'Help!'* I linked, in panic. *'Can't breathe.'*

My skin stiffened. My sinuses became lanced with pain. I screwed my eyes shut, terrified that they would explode from the lack of exterior pressure. Rough hands were trying to wrap me in insulfoam and, still under the mod's influence, I stupidly fought with someone trying to shove an air mask on my face.

Then a new voice linked to me. *'Hold—hold on, partner. Help is—'*

*'Kid! Are you all right?'*

The pipeline plumbers were carrying me back to the terminal hatch. I could see Crusher's ship slowly struggle up through the thin atmos, wavering, pulsing brightly once—a shrinking light that seemed to blink out of existence. Then I heard the frenzied scraps of the noise and music for the first time and fell into blissful unconsciousness…

⁊ↄↄ

Slowly, Wolf's memories became replaced by reality again, and he slipped out of report mode.

He sat up and blinked, rubbing the back of his neck where the greatest concentration of chemicals had made contact with his skin. It felt hot and tight—a little like the UV burn under the dressing on his right ear.

Doc Pat was still in her chair. The darkness of the room complimented her skin, making her almost invisible. "All right, Wolf. I think that's enough. I wanted you to re-experience those events more for self-awareness, rather than for my review." She took his hands and held them warmly as she spoke. "Now, you told me yesterday that, in addition to the noise and music, you also hear Jonny's voice. What is he saying to you?"

"I—I don't know, Doc." Wolf still felt a bit dazed by the treatment. "It's just…words. Do you think I'm somehow reliving his death? He was following my orders when he died. Hell, he was linked to me. Maybe there's something…special about the Link that even you don't know."

Doctor Pat was a trained psychiatrist, a veteran of the Belt War and Wolf's mentor and employer at Tripleye. She looked at him and tapped her teeth with a brown fingernail.

"Maybe," she said, "but I don't think so, Wolf. As far as we know, the Link is a virus that creates a neural sympathy between several hosts. There's never been any indication that it can function without a living source. That's why we can't use computers or other mechanical devices to expand the transmission. Besides, how do you explain the fact that none of the rest of the ops hears the voice, even when they're linked?"

Wolf thought for a moment and shook his head. "I don't know, Doc. But what if the kid's not really dead? I mean, not completely—" Immediately, he knew how absurd that must sound. Communication with the dead was a thing of fantasy. Doc always sought to root things in reality. It would be different if she took the link, he thought, and then he wondered why she never did. Viralphobia?

"Level with me, Doc," he said with great care. "Am I losing it?"

Doctor Pat sighed. "You check out perfectly fine, Wolf, both psychologically and physiologically. There's not a thing wrong with you except a slight lesion on the side of your right ear. We all attended Jonny's funeral and have had come to terms with his death. Jonny's remains went back into the eco-bank at MediCen. He's only a memory, now. You have to accept that." She made a note in his file. "I think, Wolf, what you need is a healthy dose of reality. Something to keep your mind on the present. I'm taking Chico off the Link Central. I know you two get along very well together. She'll be working with you as backup."

"Thanks Doc," Wolf said, but his eyes still searched the psychiatrist's dark features for an answer. "If I'm not crazy, then—"

Doctor Pat spoke calmly, scanning through her notes. "This is very much like the time when your father died," she said. "You wouldn't let go then either."

Wolf remembered how a group of miners had been trapped during a quake near the old Tripleye offices. His father had gone to help them out. Wolf was recovering from the effects of the mod operation when he got the news that his old man had been trapped in a crevice during an aftershock.

"When I took over the agency from you in '93, the city had cited you twice for financial contempt. Debts had piled up to the surface domes, and your physical and mental states were equally disturbing. All of Achilles was happy to see me buy you out. Since then, I've structured the agency back into the relatively healthy financial state it was in when your father died. And you've come a long way, too."

"Save the lecture for someone who gives a crap."

"But you can't let yourself slip back, now," the psychiatrist went on. "It's up to you, Wolf. You've the potential to be the best damn investigator in the System. All you need to do is ignore the negative baggage you're carrying around. With a little determination and time, I'm sure the voice, or noise, or whatever will go away. It's your decision."

Wolf got up and put on his jacket. '*She's giving me the old pep talk,*' he linked to Chico. '*What do you think?*'

'*Listen to her,*' Chico responded. '*She's the best there is, and besides, she's the boss.*'

Wolf shifted his weight uneasily. Doc's mind seemed made up. If he pressed the subject any further, she would probably start talking early retirement. "Okay," he said. "I'll work on it."

"Fine," the woman answered, filing her notes away. "I'm eager to things back to normal." She gestured at the right side of Wolf's head. "How's the ear?"

He reached up and touched the medicinal patch. "Okay, I guess. The doctors at MediCen say I'll still be able to hear with it, but I'll have a scar at least ten centimeters long." Doc Pat removed the patch and inspected the burn. "They called it six tricks...or something."

"A cicatrix." The black woman smiled, tossing the bandage into the trash. "It's old French, Wolf. I think it means 'scar,'" she said, stepping back. "It suits you."

Wolf put on his hat and opened the door to the passageway. "Thanks, again, Doc."

"Take care, Wolf."

He stopped into the main concourse and touched the side of his head where the scar was developing, the cicatrix that he would carry the rest of his life.

He took a deep breath and the music came to him again, faintly. He thought he heard the voice call his name—his real name, the one nobody else ever used.

'*Don't worry, Dan,*' Jonny said. '*I'm still with you, partner, and you're still the greatest.*'

Then Wolf lost it in the rhythmic throbbing of his own pulse. He sighed. "So are you, kid."

And with abrupt determination, he tipped his Fedora and slipped in a jazzblues mod, letting the lonely strains of "Street Scene" carry him away from there.

# CHAPTER 2

*IDEE FIXE*

Believe me, Patricia, having children is not all that it's cracked up to be. Mine haven't contacted me in thirty years," Professor Selena Mishko said. She was the administrative head of Triage Foundation, the only medical research facility beyond Mars.

"No," Pat Emory said, feeling her face grow warm with embarrassment. "Children, or rather my lack of them, aren't the problem."

"Well, I haven't got all day," Mishko said. "In a few minutes, my lungs will weaken again and I'll have to re-pressurize the room. Out with it, girl, before you have to leave!"

Ever since the accident, Professor Mishko had been confined to her private lab, a hodge-podge clinic funded by various humanitarian resources and cloistered far beneath the cinder-like surface of Ceres. There, among the cloying odors of lubricating oil, sterilizing solution, and human sweat, hundreds of Outer Planet refugees who were wounded, infected, and unbalanced since the Belt War came for care and comfort, while the silver-haired woman secretly tested the bio-mechanics of the Link.

"I've encountered something unusual," Pat said, "about the Link's ability to transfer thought."

Professor Mishko leaned forward with interest. The Link was the renowned micro-virologist's greatest achievement, a variation of the communications virus she'd developed during the war to help coordinate the cultures of Titan, Europa, and the other Outer Planets. Once assimilated, this viral-soup permitted limited self-control of the body's neuro-electrical impulses. The firing of all axions at the same instant freed the mind, while stunning the body, creating a selective telepathic link between similar hosts.

"One of my ops, Wolf Archerson," Doc Pat said, "was on the Link when his partner died. Later, Wolf complained of mentally 'hearing' unusual noises and even random phrases in the other man's voice."

"What did the voice say?" Doctor Mishko rose gracefully from her bed. She dipped her feet into a pair of warm slippers and shuffled to the other end of the laboratory to adjust a dial on an electron-microscope.

Pat followed, holding out the older woman's robe.

"Apparently, nothing comprehensible, but you see the implication—if my op is sane."

Doctor Mishko shrugged into the robe and turned, looking intently into her companion's eyes. "And, is he sane?"

"Selena, I'm a trained psychiatrist."

"You're also the patient's friend and employer, and you haven't answered my question."

"Yes. I believe he's sane."

The older woman shut down the EM scope and prepared to extract the sample. "Well, Patricia," she said, "you've presented me with quite a curious problem."

"The patient seems fixated on the idea that a transient message was sent at the moment of the other man's death and somehow created a sort of communication in his head."

"Hmmm…rattling around, as it were," Mishko mused. "He's probably feeling guilty for the other man's death."

"That's what I thought. Either that, or else—"

The elderly woman placed the sample under a molecular analog field and began to review its data on the computer screen. "There is still much we don't know about the effects of the Link. I suspect that in the long-run all those neuro-electrical firings may weaken a person's memory. What you've presented to me will certainly bear looking into, Patricia. But, right now, I want you to study something else." She indicated the design on the screen.

Her breathing was becoming more labored. Pat would soon have to leave the room, so Mishko could increase the atmospheric pressure in order to be comfortable. "I've cultivated the virus that caused your sterility. Watch what happens when I expose it to 500 rads of mumeson."

Doctor Mishko pressed a key and the magnified tetra-structures on the screen began to decay. Within eight seconds, they had crumbled into a pile of inert peptides.

"My god," Pat breathed. "You've found it—a cure!"

"We can irradiate the virus within you, but—with a bath of this radiation, I'm afraid—there is only a fifty-percent chance you would survive."

"But Selena, it's still a cure!" Pat said, hugging the older woman. "You've given me hope after all these years, hope that I can be normal and conceive—"

"If you survive, Patricia. I know this is something you've been wanting for a long time, but you need to think about what will happen if the treatment is fatal, not just successful."

The Vax went breep, and Doctor Mishko moved to answer it, while taking oxygen from a tank near her bed.

Pat was awash with conflicting emotions. She sat on a lab stool and put her fingers to her temples. Children. At last, she had a slim chance of being a normal woman again and bearing warm, wonderful children. It was something she had wanted for a long time. The old girl must have been working on this for years. Typical of her to keep it a secret.

"Patricia," Mishko called.

"Oh, I'm sorry. What is it?"

The woman handed Pat a Vax copy, which read: "Urgent you return here at once. The gov is trying to shut down investigations agency. St. Mathew."

જ્જ

The doors slid shut and sealed. Pat looked around and counted eleven other passengers in the automated shuttle. Her military status had gotten her a priority seating at one of the computer access stations, where she planned to review her notes on the Link, while keeping her mind off the hard vacuum outside the ship's hull.

A boring recorded voice intoned the standard safety precautions and announced that the shuttle was ready to depart. Ceres was in relative opposition, so the trip back to Mars would only take thirteen hours.

As the macrogauss system began to repel the vessel from the asteroid's surface, Pat settled into her seat and dropped a chip into the comstation, trying not to think about her fear. After almost a decade of command during the Belt War, she still needed something solid and substantial to occupy her mind while traveling through empty space.

Well, she had plenty to think about during this trip.

Her fingers stroked the keys, adding new notes to the file she'd revised on the trip out, but her thoughts kept drifting back to Selena's discovery. The policy of Earth military personnel to accept temporary sterilization had permanently affected Lieutenant Pat Emory when she had begun active service. War was no place for pregnancy and the military was no place for children. One of the attractions of the Interplanetary Marines was that its selective virus sanctioned safe sex, replacing the potential of a growing fertilized egg with a benign neoplasm. Only, in Pat's case, it hadn't been benign.

Seventeen years ago, she had accepted the treatment that was still active within her today. Since the day she'd retired from military duty, all attempts to eliminate it had failed. The virus had mutated into a tenacious parasite which blocked her ovaries' normal function, robbing her of any chance of naturally bearing children. No other cases like hers were on record. Patricia had decided to settle "out of court," receiving from the Innerplanet Government sufficient credits to establish her psychiatric offices and investigations business in Achilles, but it was small compensation.

At the time of the attack on Ceres, during the Belt War, Selena and Chico had been perfecting and refining the use of another virus, which they called the Link. Pat immediately understood the potential for such a telepathic substance, if it could be tamed, for advancements in her psychiatric work. Imagine being able to actually read your patient's mind, in order to immediately discover the knots in logic, the obsessions, the hidden mental traumas that were sometimes all but impossible to expose, let alone treat! The Link's ability to connect the thoughts of its hosts meant that the two or even three minds could exchange information immediately, with only one drawback.

As the axions fired in each hosts' brain, the bodies were hit with a stunning blast of bio-electrical energy creating a near-epileptic seizure. The subject could survive the attack, but the long-range effects were still unknown. In addition, many individuals had proven to be allergic to the substance. Still, Pat saw in it a vast potential, and had successfully petitioned the Martian Government to permit her exclusive use of the Link in both her psychiatric and investigative businesses.

A small chime sounded in Doc Pat's temporal implant. Almost on Pavlovian cue, her stomach began to growl. She rose from the comstation and stretched.

The shuttle had passed the midpoint of its journey. Pat purposely avoided the portholes, averting her eyes to the deck, rather than gazing into the empty blackness of space. She was a grounddog, not a spacedog, and she knew it.

Typically, the choice of shuttle food was terrible—microwaved hegenbergers and fibersteak. Pat selected and prepared a tube of Napa Valley tea, drinking it and munching on a breadfruit bar she'd purchased at the Triage Foundation.

Passengers were now permitted to send and receive calls to Achilles, provided they could afford the expense. Pat attempted to reach Arthur, in order to get more info on the supposed takeover, but his office said that he was out, so she returned to her notes.

*If I were on the Link now*, she thought, *I could reach Chico or any of my executive ops*. It bothered her that she avoided using the substance. She convinced herself that it had something to do with maintaining a control factor, or avoiding a doctor being her own patient. But was it really caution, or cowardice? The substance had proved invaluable in the day-to-day operations of an investigations agency. Chico had, of course, been quite accustomed to drinking a ten-milliliter solution of it every three days.

But the latest indication unnerved her even more. Wolf was beginning to claim that the Link let him communicate with the dead! Jonny's death had been a sudden and horrible tragedy. Without any warning, a mazer rifle had cooked and sliced him. And, because the boy had been linked to Wolf at the time, the old op was afraid that somehow their two minds had been combined permanently in death. Pat doubted this, but there was still so much she didn't know about the Link's operation. Part of her regretted ever having used the substance, but what was done was done, and its positive results were working wonders for the detective agency.

Except that one of her ops, St. Mathew, had just reported that the gov was trying to shut down Tripleye. Had they found out about the exported credits to Triage? If so, wouldn't Arthur McBain have contacted her direct to discuss the problem?

Perhaps, it had something to do with their latest investigation into the Weave Corporation. Representatives from that company were known to have associated with the team of weapons thieves who had caused Jonny's death.

Doc Pat decided to place a call to St. Mathew for more information. Then she realized that the shuttle had started its incline into the Martian g-well. Thoughts swirled in her mind as the ship bucked in the thin carbon dioxide atmos—the problems with the agency, the problems with the Link, and the anticipation of a possible end to her infertility, all failed to block the palm-sweating fear of an automated landing.

Pat clinched her teeth and didn't let go until she heard the computer announce, "Transhuttle Spaceways welcomes you to Marsport Achilles. Please prepare for customs and decontamination."

∽∾∽∾

The executive ops of Tripleye filtered into the meeting room. Wolf took off his hat and hung it on the hook by the door. The short, slightly overweight man used to own and manage the agency. Pat had kept most of the furnishings as they were when she had bought him out.

Chico Kim came in, her arms full of a file containing several ledgers and Vax reports. Chico appeared to have been working steadily in the office for the last twenty hours. Her attention to detail was, at times, almost obsessive, but this was one instance when Pat was glad the oriental woman had stayed on the job.

Intensive Investigations, Incorporated, had been founded over thirty years ago as the first business of its kind on Mars. When Tripleye had fallen on hard times, Doctor Pat had acquired it to supplement her psychiatric office, on the assumption that troubled people often found the cause of their trouble in their external, as well as internal, reality.

*Besides*, Pat thought, *I always wanted to be a part of a real private investigations agency. No doubt it was due to the years I watched my mother working on the Atlanta Police Force.* And the company did make good from its gov contracts.

Pat could then channel part of the income back to Mishko at the Triage Foundation for further research on the Link. So it all balanced out and made a comfortable and logically satisfying circle.

The small room was already becoming crowded when Jules St. Mathew breezed through the door and casually threw his lean, muscular frame into a chair, stretching his legs out under the table. He looked bored, but then St. Mathew *always* looked that way whenever Pat called a meeting of her ops.

Wolf fired a sarcastic comment at St. Mathew. "Did ya have a little trouble getting out of bed, this morning?"

St. Mathew fielded the barb deftly. "I wasn't in bed, old sock." He smiled. And then his face became stony, and Pat knew he was linking to Chico whose features also stiffened momentarily.

Chico blushed and Wolf began to fume.

"All right," Pat said, to avoid a confrontation.

St. Mathew put his hand behind his long blond head of hair and yawned. *The insufferable egotist acts like he doesn't care what happens*, Pat thought. *Still, he'd been concerned enough to have sent the Vax to me Ceres.* Pat knew from his private analysis sessions that this bravado was all an act. Jules St. Mathew was, surprisingly, her most insecure operative. He was also her luckiest.

"We received the notification right after you left," he said, gesturing to the official letter Pat had already read, which stated that the agency owed close to forty thousand credits in back taxes. The charge was absurd, but Pat worried it might lead to a gov investigation into her off-planet investments.

"Did anyone contact McBain?" she asked. Arthur McBain was the government liaison who had arranged Tripleye's sanction to experimentally use the Link. He was also one of Doc Pat's closest and oldest friends. McBain and his daughter, Nancy, had lived in the old neighborhood near Stone Mountain where Pat had grown up.

"I called him right away," St. Mathew said. "He claims that his hands are tied and that a full audit is scheduled which will probably shut us down."

"That's when we decided to send you the Vax," Chico added.

Wolf looked at the two other ops and growled, "We? What's this 'we' shit?"

Chico shook her head. "Calm down, Wolfy. You were out, and I was the only one in the office when St. Mathew made the call."

St. Mathew smiled at Wolf and then winked.

Doc Pat cut in before the older detective could explode. "Stop it, you two. This is very serious. If we don't respond immediately, and in a mature manner, the company could lose its charter, to say nothing of our gov contracts. Chico, we need to file an injunction, right away. Why are you smiling, for heaven's sake?"

The Korean woman nodded to St. Mathew.

"Ah, I get it," Pat said. "You're already ahead of me, right?" Regardless of his attitude, Jules was a professional. Pat knew he cared about the agency's future as much as she did.

"I took care of it this morning," St. Mathew said, gesturing. "There's a copy in the file."

"Say?" Wolf questioned. "Who's in charge around here, anyway?"

"Hang on," Pat said, raising a palm and studying the document. "Very nice, Jules. This buys us a little time, but I'll need to refile it properly, since you forged my signature. It'll be too easy to prove I was off-planet at the time. Someone is coming down hard on us, people, and we can't afford any mistakes."

"Where's Von Roon now?" Pat asked.

"On his way back to Earth. And the mini-shuttle that Crusher escaped in is now docked at Vegas. The military traced it there, but couldn't find Crusher, or the canister, or even the modified mazer weapons. You know how easy it is to get laundered in a place like Vegas."

Pat nodded. Vegas was a pleasure port, a border town in a relatively stable LeGrange point were the marines had gone for R and R during the war. Thousands thronged there each year and lost millions to the gambling and fantasy-analysis games. Its gov and security forces were the most corrupt in the system. You could buy almost anything there and have a hell of a good time doing it. If you survived.

A second Vax on a shelf where Chico usually worked went breep.

"Don't answer it," Pat told the other woman. "Just get a copy. We don't want to be disturbed." She went back to studying the video of Von Roon. "Weave Corp was rumored to have manufactured the magnetic mines used during the Belt War," she mused. "They're one of those old-line Earth corporations that have a finger into everything."

"That's not all," Chico said, handing Doc the Vax copy. "Arthur McBain thinks they are the ones quietly lobbying the gov to initiate our tax audit."

Pat looked directly at St. Mathew.

The man shrugged nonchalantly. "So, I asked him to check."

Pat took a deep breath. "Okay. Here's how we're going to play this one. Chico, place a call to Blue Star and tell them we've got a lead on their missing…stuff. Get Tripleye a quick-contract to investigate and safeguard BSI's corporate offices and research center. That'll be your job, Wolf. When you get there, quote them a rock-bottom price. We don't want to lose this assignment."

Wolf consulted the mod in his head. "They operate one of the geothermal stations down in Dirttown. Don't you think we ought to have someone there, just in case? These are nasty guys we're dealing with. Believe me, I know."

"Those sites are already protected by the city cops," Pat said. "And Weave Corp probably got all it wanted out of BSI when that Crusher person snatched the black can-ister. But I'll keep the thought in mind." She turned her attention to another agent. "Jules, you're going to Ve-gas." The man smiled coolly. She shook her head. "I want you to find out where Crusher went, and let us know, via the Link, if you can, where to find BSI's—"

"Snot?" he asked.

She nodded. "And no gambling, or whoring. Understand?"

St. Mathew raised his eyebrows and placed his fingers on his chest, as if to say, "Who? Me?"

The other three members of the team frowned in unison.

"Yes, you!"

The meeting started to break up. Doc held them together for one more comment. "I don't think I have to tell you what this means. It's not just our little company that's involved. We're into something big—just how big is the first thing we need to find out. Don't take any unnecessary chances. Chico, I'm afraid you'll need to stay here and help me get the files in order for the audit. You'll also need to run Central for Wolf and Jules. I'll deal with our other clients, and it might be a good idea to check BSI's geothermal station, after all. The rest of you report back here as soon as you learn anything new. Questions?"

"Nope," St. Mathew said and left the room without another word.

Wolf grabbed his hat. "Piece of cake."

Pat shut off the video on the Vax and handed the chips and papers to Chico. Everything was happening too quickly. Pat hadn't had to handle this much trouble in a long time.

"Thanks, Chico."

"Uh, Doc…" the woman asked. "Under the circumstances, don't you think you should maybe be on the Link? You can coordinate operations a lot better when you can reach us all telepathically."

Pat considered her options. Why was she afraid of the Link? Because it might expose her innermost thoughts? Undermine her position of authority within the agency? Hurt her in some way, as the military's sterility virus had? She'd functioned well without it, up to now, but the current circumstances were becoming extreme. Someone was trying to shut down her company, and maybe a whole lot more.

The Link was a virus, and years ago another virus had denied her the ability to conceive, but now things had started to improve on that front and her avoidance of the Link began to feel like a silly *idee fixe*. She had just told her ops not to take any unnecessary chances. Which action posed the greatest risk: to take the Link, or not?

"I—I don't know," she said. "I'll have to think about it."

ↄ◌ↄ

*There are all sorts of sciences*, Patricia reflected. *Clean and quiet psychiatry, delicate and careful research and hot, gritty, noisy industrial mechanics.* Here at the Blue Star geothermal site, Pat was quickly awed by the enormous laser-drilling, pressure-heating, microwave-

melting, refuse-consuming and radiation-burning operations.

All around her in the huge cavern were dirty and
grumbling sub-stations designed to burn trash, melt plastic, pump vents to the center of the planet and back, receive hot gases, operate turbines, exchange heat through
fluids, and generate megavolts of radioactive power to
continue operations during an emergency, or crisis.

The facility—one of three which supplied electricity
and heat to all of Achilles City—was packed with rubble,
noise, filth, and the combined odors of rock dust, ozone,
and human sweat, only a portion of which seemed partly
blocked by the helmet and air filters Pat wore as she
picked her way through the messy installation. This was
certainly a science far removed from her quiet offices
dedicated to cultivated psychiatry and deductive logic.

The raw heat was the first force to offend her. Achilles was in some respects a giant spaceship, self-contained
in its manufactured environment. To get to this location,
Pat had passed through one of the city's vast greenhous-
es—a better description would be hot-houses—that lay
adjacent to the geotherm station.

The humid temperature there must have been set in
the high eighties—encouraging for plant growth, but
withering for humans. After walking through this jungle,
she had arrived at the relatively cooler Blue Star Industries power station, but Operations Manager Duke Lexington wasn't in his office.

He had gone out to the drilling site to settle a dispute and get work started up again.

Pat had been given a helmet and directions to the operations area. Shielded somewhat from the chorus of physical forces around her, she picked her way through the chaotic-seeming facility. At last she came upon a group of workers standing near the edge of a wide bore hole. "Excuse me. Is there a Mr. Lexington here?"

The group turned to look at her. Most of the helmets they wore were covered with graffiti, except for the face-plates.

"Yeah? Who are you?" a large, dark-skinned man replied.

Doc was impressed with the looks of this fellow. "I'm the special security guard from Tripleye," she said. "Your main office sent me down to keep an eye on things."

The big man laughed and the other workers joined in. Pat could see that several of the workers were women, and since Lexington's skin was as black as hers, Pat decided the derisive laughter wasn't sexism, or racism, but a class reaction, designed to challenge an outsider. These tough, sweat-collar workers were putting her through a mild group-bonding test, so she added, "I'm Lieutenant Commander Pat Emory, IPMC, retired."

That got her nothing but silence. Which, possibly, was the right response.

Op Manager Lexington turned back to address his

workers. "Okay, Lucky, you get the picture. I want this well capped off in forty-eight hours. Now get your crew moving, or you're all history." Then he started walking away and called back to Pat, "Come on."

She stepped up her pace to reach the man. This was not the way she planned to conduct the interview.

"Mr. Lexington—"

"Call me Duke, Commander."

She drew abreast of him, nearly tripping on a valve that ran across their pathway. "Hold it, Duke. Where are we going in such a hurry?"

The man stopped, turned, and looked at her through his visor. "You know anything about geotherm operations?"

"A little," she answered, adding quickly, "but I could stand to learn more."

Duke nodded. "Then let's take a quick tour."

They worked their way through the facility for the next few minutes. It seemed to Pat that the operation had something to do with microwaving oil and plastic refuse, until it became a hot liquid. Then it was pressurized through a lock that led into a borehole that sent the gunk down almost three klicks to the Martian magma where it became a gas. The expanding fluid shot up a depressurized vent and gave off its heat through a series of exchangers, while driving a row of turbines to produce electricity.

"Co-generation," Duke said, as they stood on a platform over the pressure lock. "Nearly a third of an exa-joule each year from the combined heat transfer and electricity. And the other two plants run by our competitors do the same."

"You must be putting out more power than the launch accelerators on the surface," Pat guessed.

"A whole lot more. Our electrical generating capacity is nearly 1000 megawatts. Let's go down for a closer look." The man stepped into a wire cage that ran along a track up and down the outer surface of the pressure lock.

"Wha—what?"

"Come on," he said, gesturing. "It's all part of the job."

*Bull shit*, she thought. *This is another test. He must be awfully insecure to need to play these silly games.* Nonetheless, she carefully stepped onboard, and he closed the cage door while activating the pulley engine. They descended slowly past the side of the pressure lock.

"What's this for again?" she asked, as the rough wall of rock seemed to press in toward the lock's metal surface.

"The melted plastic would start to harden again, if we didn't keep it under heavy pressure. If it became solid, it wouldn't flow down to the magma, would it?"

Pat looked up. The wide opening at the top of the hole was rapidly dwindling, and darkness closed in around them. "How deep do we go?"

Duke shrugged. "Only a kilometer," he said, switching on the light in his helmet.

Doc swallowed and fumbled to turn on her light, as well. It was getting hotter and harder and harder to catch her breath. No, this was definitely not at all the interview that she'd imagined on the way to the site. Sweat rolled off her body in steaming trickles now. Duke Lexington didn't seem to mind at all. He was casually talking to someone on his helmet's portable comunit which bulged next to "Born to Bore" graffiti.

Finally, Pat could see the bottom of the hole coming up to meet them. And, within minutes, they were back on solid ground, albeit a lot lower than she preferred.

"Okay," he said, getting out. "We can talk safely in here."

"Safely!" Pat yelped. "Next time, buster, we're meeting in my office. That's safe enough for me."

"So, what's the story?" Lexington asked. "Why does the company need special security ops? Somebody think my people are spying for the competition?"

Doc stayed in the elevator cage. "This is just a routine investigation," she said. "And, I can conduct it better on the surface. I mean in the cavern. Oh hell, can we get out of here, or do you have some deep-seated paranoia about losing your job?"

Lexington came back into the cage. She suddenly noticed a strong sexual attraction to the man. "Look whose paranoid," he said, starting the pulley engine.

The cage slowly crept up the track.

Contrary to her confidence facade, Pat often struggled to handle stress gracefully. Growing up fatherless in the urban Stone Mountain, daughter of an Atlanta patrolwoman, the young, olive-skinned girl had supplemented her income with a ROTC scholarship, while working hard to graduate from Georgia Tech class of '87 with a degree in Advanced Psychiatry. Her knowledge of human nature was put to the test during final training at the IMPC's Camp Lejeune. She'd received a lieutenancy and was assigned to the psycho-ward on Elsix, a confusing and frustrating job.

Then she'd run afoul of General Carver who didn't care for the style of her de-stress conditioning of his troops. He claimed that "the irresponsible comments of a black corpman during time of war" undermined his troops' fighting spirit and contributed to their poor morale during the Battle of Io.

Doc Pat was soon reassigned to the front lines, where she experienced first-hand the etiological factors of battle fatigue while fighting for her life near Ceres. Remarkably, she held her own against the "Outies" until the war was over, not only surviving, but gaining the rank of lieutenant commander before taking early combat retirement at the age of twenty-nine.

It was while she was stationed in the Belt, during a rush evacuation of the Triage facility, due to an "Outie" mining operation, that she met the famous micro-virologist, Doctor Mishko. For nearly three centuries, mankind had successfully mined the asteroids, but the "Outie" terrorists gave new meaning to the phrase when they introduced their magnetic explosive drones into the crowded and chaotic Belt. Pat's troops had to constantly sweep the area around the inhabited planetoids in order to locate and de-activate the deadly devices.

During the evacuation, Dr. Selena Mishko and her assistant, Chico Kim, became trapped in an airless passageway. Pat helped rescue them, and Chico had quickly recovered. But the lack of oxygen together with poisonous gases from the mines permanently destroyed sixty-five percent of Mishko's lung tissue, leaving her to live the rest of her life in a pressure suit, or a specially constructed room. Thinking of it now reminded Pat of the stressful pressure in her own chest. *Why am I so uncomfortable down here? Is it this man, or more of my viral-phobia?*

Then, suddenly, the cage stopped in its tracks.

Duke tried to restart the engine, but there was no response.

"What's wrong?" she asked.

He only grunted and quickly placed a call from his comunit.

Pat's anxiety grew. *This is only a psychophysiological response*, she told herself, as the pressure on her chest seemed to increase.

"We've been having a little trouble with power outages," Lexington supplied. "The emergency nuclear generator has been activated. We should be moving again in a few seconds."

*Small comfort*, Pat thought. *If I were on the Link, I could send for help. How can I afford to let my own selfish fixations jeopardize the agency's future? I've got to overcome this for the good of my team.*

The car lurched as it began ascending. Pat looked up at the tiny light source at the top of the hole, and thanked God.

After want felt like hours later, they were back in the cavern where Duke immediately called for a meeting to investigate the power outage. Pat spent the rest of the day learning about geotherm operations and examining different causes for the drops in power. No clear mechanical source for the outages could be identified. That meant that some human factor must be involved. The station employed over three hundred on-site personnel, and all of them had been loyal to the company for several generations. It was unlikely, therefore, that any of them would sabotage BSI's operations and risk a drastic change in their lifestyle.

So, what did that leave? All Pat knew was that she was flat-out tired after a demanding day in this hell hole. Finding that she could no longer think straight, she wearily shuffled back through the hot house and caught a ground shuttle out of Dirttown to her apartment near the center of Achilles. Granting herself the luxury of a real shower with real water, she relaxed and fell exhausted into bed.

ⱨⱨⱨ

Now that there was a faint possibility that she could conceive and bring a child into the world, Pat ruminated over her own childhood in the USA. Looking back, it no longer seemed as trying as she once remembered it. It had been an awkward time for relationships with boys, what with her job, her schooling and the responsibility of looking after her sister, Amber. And her mother had worked a lot of third shift, serving and protecting the streets of Atlanta, as part of the area's police force. But life is almost always simpler when you're young and educable.

Arthur McBain was the only person in Achilles who had known her back then. He and his daughter, Nancy, whom Pat only vaguely remembered, had immigrated to Mars, while Pat had been stationed near Io. Nancy's tale was one of un-even success.

The owner of the House of Holos, Adam Wu sold a new business concept to the VideoMars theater chain. Together, they sponsored a "Miss Mars" contest. The finalists were auditioned and a CDVax was cut and placed on the end of a series of popular concert programs. The viewers voted Nancy the winner. She and her father came to Mars, so she could play a lead part in the "Captain Columbus" series. Eventually, Nancy met and secretly married Vax executive John America, and returned to Earth. But Arthur remained behind, working as part of the gov's Permit and Contract Department. Ever since then, Arthur had looked fondly after the "stoic, little girl" whom his daughter had once known.

Pat suspected that there was more to his interest than misplaced parental concern, but the man was always quite formal in all their dealings.

Arthur was in the Tripleye offices this morning, trying to straighten out the tax tangle and advise Pat of semi-classified info on Weave Corp. The heavy-set, stoop-shouldered man stood in her office, wearing an innocuous woolover two-piece suit of dark blue that made his rust-colored skin look old and worn. The wire-rimmed glasses, perched on the end of his flat nose, reminded Pat of the man's affinity for antiques. He was a self-centered yet humble individual, and he knew more about Gov operations and politics than anyone she had ever met. She wished he would just take care of the whole mess.

"Now, you're going to have to produce records showing full income during the buyout procedure. The annuity from the IPMC, any windfall or gambling profits, income from gov contracts and inheritances, plus the normal profit from the psychiatry and investigations businesses…"

Pat had a difficult time following the instructions. Her mind was on the Link. She looked at Chico tapping away at a data program, trying to get answers that would help keep the business free from gov control. Wolf, Jules, and the others were all on the job, standing double duty. Why did Pat think she could continue to harbor her prejudices when the others were pulling more than their fair share? They could get so much more done, and it would re-knit the spirit between her and her ops. *Besides, what's another virus, anyway?*

Okay, so a virus had hurt her once, taken away the possibility of her ever having a child naturally. She could always try an embryo-plant, but that just wouldn't be the same. *I want my own child, not someone else's.* So, there it was. Her problem was only partly physiological. Her own psychological attitudes were keeping her from living the life that had lately become an obsession. All she had to do was change her mind-set, and doors would open all around her. And that moment yesterday in the pit had proven how foolish her fears were.

"Are you listening, Patricia?" he asked. The centers of his eyes seemed solid black and the whites were lined with red from decades' attention to detail.

"Oh—sorry, Arthur." She sighed. "I appreciate your help, but I had a rough day, yesterday. And there's a lot happening in my life just now. Chico helps on the accounts: maybe she can show you what you're after. I'm terribly tired."

"Young lady—" Of course, no one else would ever think of referring to Pat in those words. "—you've got to a part of this. I see that I'll have to do something dramatic to impress upon you the enormity of your situation."

Pat made a skeptical expression.

"How does this grab you?" he asked. "Weave Corp is trying to gain a fifty-one percent ownership of Achilles Municipal Management."

The statement caught Pat's interest. "They're trying to buy the city? Keep talking."

"Well, it's not all together certain, but the indications are that Von Roon would like to see the current management group fail, so he can come in and incorporate. He holds the ticket on basic investments, or at least his company does. It seems Achilles's founders signed a non-bankruptcy agreement decades ago that made the city a Donor World. If it doesn't show a profit, the note comes due and the lender corporation can liquidate it as it sees fit."

"And Weave Corp is the lender."

"Not, originally, but—"

"But Von Roon managed to maneuver into that position," Pat mused. "And, now he wants to take over operations. But that's insane. The people would never stand for it."

"Well, he won't shut the city down, because he knows it can be made to turn a profit, but he might bleed it to a slow death, or make some sweeping restructure operations that are more suiting to his personal interests."

"But why chase after my little business?"

"Because, young lady, you've interfered with his plans. And, you still are, I imagine. Von Roon is a very forceful man. Did you know that he's also the head of the Neo-Socialist party? You don't get to a position like that without being a power to be reckoned with."

"Keep talking, Arthur. You've succeeded in capturing my full attention."

"Well, the Neo-Socialists were a splinter group of the Democracy versus Communism struggles of the twentieth century. The group managed to limp along during the twenty-first, due to the combined forces of planetary expansion and conflicts like the Belt Wars, which fostered intense planetary pride. Finally, with the Great Crazie Days of the turn of this century, Von Roon started to move the party and his Corp closer and closer together, until now he's perhaps the most politically powerful individual on Earth."

"I wondered," Pat said, "why such an important man would take the time from his busy schedule to come all the way out to Mars. He was looking over his prospective purchase." She pressed a key on the Vax, saying, "Chico?"

The oriental woman's voice came back after a few seconds. "Yes, Doc?"

"I want you to research the data banks for info on the Neo-Socialists." Pat looked at Arthur, who nodded. "I seem to remember something way back about a psychiatrist named Jung, so you might want to cross ref that, too."

Chico sighed.

"What's the matter?" Pat asked.

"I don't think you realize how much work you've given me already, Doc. Preparing for this audit is a fulltime job, and I've got to keep in contact with the other ops—"

"I'm sorry, Chico. You're right," Pat answered. It wasn't like Chico to complain, but these were extreme circumstances. Perhaps they were affecting Chico as much as her boss. "Arthur McBain is here to give us a hand with the taxes. Why don't you come into my office, while I send a note to Tamera at the data vaults. She owes me a favor, anyway."

Chico came in and quietly set up two portable data comps on the meeting room table, while Pat sent her request for info to the city's main computer bank.

"You know," Arthur said, "with a bit of luck, the Vaults might give you all the investment and tax info you need, as well."

Doc Pat cast a quizzical glance at Chico. The young, dark-haired woman nodded. "I'll get on it, right away."

Pat was a little surprised. It wasn't like Chico not to have checked such an obvious data source on her own. Something was definitely bothering the woman.

The rest of the day was filled with calculating and collating escalation and deprecation percentages, dividend compounding, net buyout averaging and corp tax discounts, until Pat's head was humming and her eyes were blurred. And this only covered the firm's first year of operation. The only respite from the brain-breaking number crunching was whenever Wolf linked in with an update from his stakeout at BSI. St. Mathew was a loner, so there would be no communications him unless he got into trouble.

"Why hasn't someone invented a program to cut through all this calculation?" Pat pleaded.

Arthur took it upon himself to answer. "Mostly, because every case is different, and your audit is the most thorough I've seen in many a year. They mean to get the forty thousand credits, or shut you down."

"Just who does this city think it is, anyway?" Doc asked, blowing off steam. "I've helped solve some of the toughest scams it's ever seen—from off-planet shuttle repos, to locating and handling dampened radio-isotopes. Remember that Warpman hostage crisis? The local security cops were too afraid to go in. Wolf and I had to talk those loonies down and all we got for our trouble were autographs and a couple of passes to the rest of the season!"

"Patricia, please," Arthur said, rubbing her shoulders to show her how much he cared. "This isn't like you. Calm down and try to deal with the situation as you would advise one of your patients."

"Thank you, Arthur," she said, rising from her chair.

"You've been a dear, as usual. But I think Chico and I can handle things until tomorrow."

He seemed disappointed. "You want me to go?"

"I'll call you." She smiled, leading the man to the office entrance. "Perhaps we can have lunch tomorrow and you can tell me all you've learned about Weave Corp."

He shrugged. "Very well, Patricia. Tomorrow, then."

They embraced, lightly.

"Good night," Pat said.

He went out the door. She moved to a locked cabinet behind her desk. Chico still tapped away at the keyboard, intent on her calculations.

Pat faced her fixation and selected one of the back-up squibs used by her ops when they were in the field and couldn't get to the office for the standard Link treatment. She placed the needle against the back of her neck, clinched her teeth, and inserted the substance into her neural system.

The room shimmered as if it were suffering the effects of a minor quake. The lights seemed to pulse with the same resonance of Pat's heartbeat, while her body froze. She heard a faint singing, or humming the way Jonny used to sound under his breath when he was intent on his music.

Chico worked at her station. Pat felt as if she could see the comp display from Chico's point of view. The numbers streamed into Pat's consciousness, filling her with all the calculations as they flashed through Chico's awareness. But there was another awareness, too. A faint, quiet contentedness, floating up from Chico, or near Chico, or in—

Pat gasped. The Korean woman stiffened. They were on the Link together. All three of them. Pat. Chico. And Chico's baby.

Pat couldn't help feeling an ironic ache of envy.

∽∾∽∾

The next morning, after having taken a full dose of the Link, Pat was back at the BSI geotherm station, ostensibly on security stakeout. What she was really doing was playing with the Link.

The psychiatric possibilities were fascinating. While it would still help patients to exorcize their inner thoughts and feelings, the attending physician would no longer have to wade through a mire of repressions. Provided the patient wasn't allergic to the Link, a correct diagnosis could be made in an instant. Doc couldn't wait to try it out on Wolf. If there were some way to loop it back to him, he'd see that his "ghostly voice" was just repressed guilt for Jonny's death.

The known uses of the Link were limited, however. Conscious thoughts were "driven" by the sender, and could be selectively directed to a receiver, only if the receiver cooperated. Once the sender stopped driving the Link, the receiver could no longer get a clear communication. Thus, when the sender was asleep or unconscious, a receiver could only pick up faint, low-grade holistic sensations, such as fear, or contentment.

Since a side effect of electro-neural linking was to "freeze" the user's nervous system with a mild seizure, exotic activities like shared sex were out. Much to St. Mathew's disappointment. High-grade stimulants and depressants muddied the reception, which helped to explain Wolf's voices, since he'd been drinking a lot of wine lately.

Doc Pat linked to Wolf and was gratified to receive a clear response.

'*What's happening at the Blue Star Corp offices?*' she asked, feeling her muscles stiffening.

'*Hi, Doc,*' Wolf linked back. '*Chico told me you'd decided to join us. Welcome aboard. I've just finished scanning one of Von Roan's recent employee relations presentations. It's kind of enlightening.*'

'*How so? God, this is fun!*'

'*Yeah. It is, ain't it? But wait until your joints start to creak. Anyway, Von Roon figures that anyone who's not with Weave Corp is "pioneer rubble."*'

'*What?*'

'*Listen, I'll read you some of the more interesting parts. "Non-members have no vision. They are unformed and lack creative spirit."*'

'*Sounds like he's a strict disciplinarian.*'

'*No shit. And get this: "Soon mankind will touch the*

*stars. We must be prepared to meet this challenge by re-maining pure and clean in mind and body. The pioneer rabble in the Belt and the Outer Planets are sub-human in their lack of planning and organization. They must not be our vanguard."'*

'*This is an employee relations speech?*'

'*Pretty weird, huh? You want more?*'

'*No,*' Pat said. '*The pain is getting too intense. But I do want you to come in next week, so we can use the Link in your therapy.*'

'*If we're still in business next week.*'

'*Uh, right. Gotta go.*'

'*Scram.*'

Pat took a deep breath and continued her security inspection of the power station's operations. She worked the stiffness out of her joints while observing the work gangs going through their routine tasks and procedures. Duke Lexington was scheduled to come into the headquarters' center in the next half hour to receive Pat's latest report. The results were not good. BSI workers were loyal with regard to the competition, but there were strong signs of other influences in their personnel lives aside from employment. Religion, for instance.

Pat decided to get an update from Chico before handing in her report. Besides, it also meant she could use the Link again.

'*Chico. How are you doing?*'

The oriental woman still seemed reserved. She

sensed Pat's envy, perhaps she still resented being stuck at Link Central. For some reason, she was cool to the subject of her baby. Pat felt uncomfortable now whenever they communicated.

*'Fine, Doc. I'm fine. I ran a cash flow analysis of the public records of Weave Corp that Arthur got for us.'*

'Yes?'

*'I'm not sure, but there seem to be some fairly large amounts of credit transferring to accounts that cross-ref with those of a few BSI employees.'*

'Payoffs?' Pat asked. *'Maybe they're bribing Blue Star Corp officials.'*

*'I—I don't know. It might just be going to middle managers, or even bonuses for workers at the geothermal station. You'd better be careful who you—'*

A sudden explosion shook the operations building, knocking Pat off her feet. She looked out a wide plex window and saw a huge gout of black steam burst up from the main vent, near the heat exchangers. Alarms rang all around her. Workers hurried in a panic to escape the rolling clouds of scalding pressurized gas.

*'Chico. We've got an A-red emergency here. Send security and rescue teams, and tell them to wear masks and shields. The entire cavern is filling with dense, black gas!'*

Pat signaled for Duke's helmet, to try and get some idea of what was happening near the explosion.

"A transformer blew up," he sneered. "Just about

ripped out the side of two heat exchangers. The gas is mostly steam mixed with a small leak from the returning oil and melted plastics. We'll need to evacuate if the cloud gets any denser."

"Was it an accident?" Pat asked. She could hardly hear Duke's reply for all the alarms going off and the roar from the disaster site.

"I'm sure it's sabotage, but how can I separate the guilty shitheads from the three hundred loyal workers?"

"I've got an idea," Pat answered, "but I'll need to use the head-display."

"Go ahead. Things couldn't be worse."

*God, I hope not*, Pat thought. There was a slight chance that what she was planning could endanger the entire facility, permanently. But, as Wolf had once told her, "Sometimes you gotta break a few heads, if you expect to crack a case."

The HD popped to life, sending Pat's voice and image to the upper of the interior of each worker's faceplate. Pat pushed the gain all the way to max. "May I have your attention, please?" she asked. "Everyone please keep calm. The situation is under control. A few uncreative and inferior persons have tried to disrupt our operations, but these weak, insipid individuals will soon learn that they little chance of success."

Pat imagined that Duke was having a fit over what she had just announced. If anything, her comments would inspire the saboteurs to further their attacks, rather than end them. But that was exactly what Pat had in mind.

Again, she made the announcement, purposely ignoring the calls from Duke and the other line operations supervisors, hoping to draw out the attackers.

She was standing stiff, linked to Chico for an update on the rescue teams when the two men came at her. Out in the cavern, every other able-bodied worker was hustling to task as emergency procedures dictated. But, within the operations office, two burly, helmeted men rushed in and took hold of Pat, knocking her unconscious with a well-placed blow to the back of the head.

When she awoke, she found that they were carrying her on a stretcher, as if she were a victim of the disaster, which in a way was true. Pat immediately linked to Chico. *'I'm in big trouble. I tried to run a bluff on the saboteurs, taunting their ideologies to draw them out, but it worked too well.'*

*'I don't understand. Where are you?'*

Pat went off Link long enough to try and get her bearings. Through the chaos and the dark clouds of gas and steam, she thought she recognized the shape of the emergency nuclear power plant. *'Dear God! I think they're going to try and take out the backup power. That will shut everything down and contaminate the entire facility. Chico, you've got to call direct to BSI. Try to get Wolf to help you. Warn them that all Achilles may be in danger.'*

Pat came off the Link to hear the two men planning to "destroy two problems with one blast." She rolled off of the stretcher, trying desperately to get her footing in the jumble of pipes and tubing that supplied the mini-reactor. One of the men grabbed at her and swung an impact hammer. "So we're weak and inferior, are we?"

"Yes," Pat grunted, bringing up a knee. She hit the man solidly in the crotch, then ripped away his mask. She wanted to gulp down a few breaths of fresh, clean air, but the other man struck her from behind.

"You filth!" he shouted. "Weave will crush all you dirty, little people."

Her head rang from the blow and her lungs screamed for clean air.

He hit her again, and through smeared vision, Pat saw him break the security seals and open the reactor's shielding. "Let's see what you look like during melt-down."

*'Chico. Wolf. They're opening the mini-reactor and releasing hard radiation.'*

*'What!'*

*'They're sacrificing themselves, like zealots, and they're taking me with them!'* Pat brought a heavy chunk of rock down hard on the back of the man's head. *'What do I do now?'*

Wolf shot her back an answer. *'I've got one of the BSI engineers here with me and he's going to tell us how to shut the reactor back down.'*

'*Thank God. What do I do?*' She felt a subtle vibration throughout her body.

For the next hellish minutes, Pat froze and linked to Wolf for instructions, then unfroze and struggled to execute the next phase of the reactor's shut down. She seemed to be trapped in a nightmare of commands and sensations. She thought she heard laughter, but the dark smoke and gas clogged her lungs; the exposure to the radiation made her body tingle; and the chaos all around her blurred her perceptions until the laughter blended in her mind with a harsh roar that turned into a pulsing music that seemed to carry a faint, but broken voice.

Then the blackness took her down.

⌘

Pat felt burning pain.

It ripped her from unconsciousness and deposited her in a clean, white hospital bed.

'*Hey, I think she's awake,*' Wolf linked.

She tried to focus on the bright light reflecting off his bald head.

"Doc?" Chico asked. "Are you okay?"

Pat wanted to answer, but her throat was a dry as Hellas Plains. Someone squirted water into her mouth, and she tried to swallow. Most of the water washed down her chin. She breathed roughly and tried to speak.

As she focused on Wolf and Chico standing over her

together, Pat immediately thought of the baby. She must have linked the thought, because Wolf asked "What baby?" and Chico shook her head in warning.

A physician passed before her vision and said something encouraging about her condition and the tests. Whatever that meant.

Pat drifted off to sleep, wondering if the gov would extend its deadline for the back taxes, now that she was hospitalized.

ᕫᔕᕫᔕ

When she awoke, they were all there again. MediCen must have been using a regular schedule of stimulants, which helped explain why everyone was on hand the moment she awakened.

Even St. Mathew was back from Vegas.

Pat tried to Link him a greeting, but found that either the Link was muddled by the medication, or it had faded without renewal.

"You stopped them," Wolf told her. "I got a rescue team to you, and that Lexington guy managed to take them out and get you to a decon station. The geothermal plant will be running at half capacity for the next few months, but you kept it from burning up half the city. You're a big busting hero!"

Pat nodded and felt a sharp pain in her side where her attacker had jabbed his foot.

"H—how bad?" she asked.

St. Mathew cleared his throat. "The doctors say you'll be up in a few more days. You took a lot of smoke and radiation. The smoke is gone and they're running scrubbers through your system every four hours. Want to hear about my trip to Vegas?"

"Did you—find any—"

"Crusher Cloud was gone, by the time I got there, but I met one of his cohorts. These are very strange people we're dealing with, Doc. They are being called Neo-Nazis, and they appear to be poised for a majority influence of Earth's Political Council. The one I met was definitely associated with Weave Corp."

Another thought drifted into Pat's consciousness. She searched Chico and Wolf's eyes. "Tax audit?"

St. Mathew held up a folder of high-denomination credits. "BSI is offering to pay our back taxes. Sort of a reward. Besides, I picked up a few extra credits while on Vegas," he smiled. There must have been over fifty thousand credits in the folder.

"Stolen?" she queried.

He laughed. "Call it a loan. From Weave Corp."

Wolf slapped the other man hard on the shoulder. "Replitroplic!"

Chico looked at Wolf questioningly.

Pat began to tire. "Have Arthur pay them direct immediately—into the gov's account."

Chico nodded. "He's scheduled to come by later for a police report."

A doctor drifted past again, this time with a small MediVax and a MediCen name badge that identified him as Harold Custer. "Commander Emory," he said, "I think I've got some good news for you. We're not entirely certain, but we think the radiation may have destroyed the virus in one of your ovaries."

Pat heart slammed in her chest. *Oh God, the mumesons—the radiation treatment Selena had cautioned me about. It worked! I'm no longer a sterile old rock.*

"You understand, it's not conclusive," the doctor warned. "But we've been in contact with your physician on Ceres, who advises that just this sort of treatment was what she had been considering, so you're a very lucky woman to have come through all of this. I must advise you to keep calm and let the treatment—"

But Pat couldn't hear him. Chico was hugging her. Wolf reached out to comfort Chico and, suddenly, they were all holding each other. That's when Pat fell into a warm and comfortable sleep.

# CHAPTER 3

*HIGH JINX*

Just below the point where the clear Liucura River entered the muddy Trancura, in a land called Chile, there lies a cool body of fresh water known as Martinez Pool. There in a tributary brook, Jules St. Mathew pretended to curl his line, snaking it out like a graceful gossamer whip, until the colorful fly settled lightly on the water's shimmering surface. He hoped it was a tantalizing morsel for some unsuspecting trout.

The serenity enfolded him, just as he had planned. Jules had chosen this reality of calm and quiet, not only to help his concentration, but to unsettle his opponent by its openness.

According to the rules of the game, Jules could pick the site, and his opponent could pick the weapons, while neither could know what the other had planned until the confrontation.

Leisurely, he backcast into the Liucura, feeling the line zing out, arcing high above the rippling water and gliding down through the morning mist to plop in the cold, dark water.

St. Mathew was relieved to be away from the Link. He took private pleasure in having gained an assignment away from the thoughts of the other operatives. He was a confirmed loner, and the mere idea of someone reading his mind made him very uneasy. He a man with many cherished secrets, and it pleased him that the other Tripleye ops weren't here on Vegas to see him play Vision Duel.

He trolled quietly in the false reality he'd created, waiting for the first appearance of his competitor. This fantasy vision of fishing in a Chilean river was quite convincing. The sun rose slowly over the gray crest of the Andes, pulling back the shadow of Villarrica's extinct peak and warming St. Mathew's back. Too bad he couldn't modify the reality to make the volcano erupt when it would be to his advantage. Ah well, if you didn't play by the rules, you didn't win.

The water gurgled and whispered. A slight breeze brushed his long, blond hair. A mosquito buzzed his left ear. No, it wasn't a mosquito. It was the visionsuit's alert signal, warning Jules that his combatant had entered the reality of the game.

Reeling in his line, St. Mathew kept a sharp eye over his shoulder.

So, where was the Italian?

He felt a tingle of excitement ripple up his spine. According to the rules of the game, the man had to initiate his attack in the next eight seconds. St. Mathew's fingers snagged and tightened the hook of the exotic fly onto the reel of his rod, and he began to wade toward shore.

The sky was clear. Jules could see a good three hundred meters all around him. There was only one place left for the attacker to hide. As St. Mathew reached the shoreline, he heard the chuckling splash behind him and turned, ducking to avoid the thrust from his opponent's foil.

*So,* he thought, *I have to fence with a fishing rod. This should be fun!*

The man rose dripping from beneath the river's surface, wearing a black tumble suit. His dark eyes were mocking and slightly wild.

Cautiously, St. Mathew watched the man step forward through the shallow water, sneering and raising his foil with his right arm, while wiping wetness from his mustache and pointed lip beard with the sleeve of his left.

Jules knew that by now the other man's viewsuit had interfaced perfectly with his own to complete the fantasy circuit. The spectators at the Home locations could now receive a combined objective view, enhanced by the game's computer as it collated the output from the two men's suits.

St. Mathew laughed and raised his fishing rod in mock salute. "Who are you supposed to be?" he asked. "Elf Fago Baca?"

The man lunged forward without a word. The tip of his sword weapon whizzed past St. Mathew's nose.

The fishing reel made a terrible guard, upsetting the balance of every thrust, but Jules counted himself lucky to even have a weapon. Before the encounter, he had no way of knowing if his opponent would be attacking with a crossbow, or a bullwhip. Vision Duel was strictly a gentleman's sport, hence electrical and ABC weapons were forbidden. This meant his attacker could use a set of brass knuckles, a sling, an arrow, or even outrageous fortune, but never gas, mazers, gunpowder, or poison. Just last year, a fellow had tried to bend the rules and dump boiling oil on his opponent, but *la regle du jeu* wouldn't allow it.

The man lunged again and Jules fell back among the gravel on the shore.

He quickly tossed away his tackle basket, wishing he had dreamt up at least one trout with which to distract his attacker. Instead, he skimmed the snow-shoe fish net at the man's head, hoping to distract him.

It was an ineffective maneuver. The man batted the net aside with his free hand and continued his advance.

Maybe a bluff would work.

With his free hand, St. Mathew found a spool of fishing line in the wide pocket of his vest. He pitched the object at his opponent's legs, yelling, "Shuriken!"

The man jump back, his feet losing their classic right-angle relationship necessary for optimum balance. Sometimes a good bluff made all the difference between winning and losing.

Jules grasped the advantage, raising his rod well above their heads, then zooming its tip downward, hoping to whip it across his combatant's eyes.

The next few minutes were a flurry of thrusts, parries, cut-overs and disengagements as the two men confronted each other up and down the shoreline. Each feint, engagement and release flashed in the morning sunlight, backlit by the sparkling river.

Jules concentrated on a series of binds and envelopments, his strong spun-carbon rod encountered the firm metal blade high, then low, then high again.

The man lunged as St. Mathew riposted, parried, and scrambled for a secondary attack.

His opponent fell to one knee, executing a full body turn, and came up on St. Mathew's blind side.

Jules somersaulted backward, hearing the rasp of the man's blade cutting the air where he had just stood.

Coming gamely into position again, both men now were breathing hard. The spectators certainly were getting their money's worth, Jules thought, as he heaved a handful of moist pebbles at his competitor's face.

The man dodged left and St. Mathew caught the tip of his opponent's foil with the sturdy monofilament of his fishing line. With a snap of the wrist and a sudden turn from the hips, Jules snatched the weapon from the other man's hand, sending it sailing up in a wide arc to land in the rushing stream with a quiet splash.

At first, his attacker stood stunned on the rocky shore. Then, without a word, he bowed deeply in honor of St. Mathew's skill.

Jules reached under his chin and lifted the visor of his viewsuit. The Chilean river scene slipped from view and he could see the gathering of spectators clustered around the one-man control chamber in the center of the casino. Taking a relaxing breath, he popped the seal and heard the wave of their exuberant voices.

"Way to go, Terego!" one guy advised, pounding Jules's shoulder.

"I knew you could take him."

"You're still the best, Al," another declared, shaking his hand.

"I never lose when I bet on you!"

Stripping away the tight, confining shirt which housed the web of neuro-muscular sensors, Jules stepped out the control chamber and met his admirers with all the gusto of a holo-vid superstar.

A shapely blonde smeared rouge on his ear with her lips. Someone handed him a drink. He poured it on the blonde woman's head, and the crowd howled in delight when she kissed him again, this time long and lustily. When it was over, he laughed in mock surrender and held out his card to receive his winnings.

His opponent—one Giuseppe Delfino in Naples—had lost over eight thousand credits and immediately filed for a rematch. According to the rules, the next time he would get to choose the site and Jules the weapons. The competition would go on as it had for nearly seven years. Starport Vegas was host to more than six hundred such tournaments every year.

Jules tried to catch his breath. He'd been lucky again, in more ways than one. Swallowing a glass of Chateau Oliver '93, he eyed the broad-shouldered man approaching from the other end of the bar.

"Mr. Terego," the man said to Jules, "that was quite impressive!"

"Thanks awfully." Jules felt his hand being shook again. "But the Italian made his first mistake coming at me from under the water. I'm sure it ruined his vision."

The man looked embarrassed. "I—I'm not with the media," he admitted.

Jules wasn't surprised. "I never said you were. I'm just making conversation, until you decide to tell me your name and trouble."

∽∾∽

Spaceport Vegas was an artificial duty-free state located in a course-corrected orbit relatively equidistant between Mars and Earth. Right now, it was in perigee with Mars, heading through a leisurely four-month cruise on its way back toward the Mother planet. On Vegas, everything was for sale, and the advertisements were everywhere.

The basic law of Vegas was the law of supply and demand, enforced by a strong, militant police agency. Originally, a stepping-off point and R'n'R facility for the Inner Planets during the Belt War, today the average vacationer could feel safe on Vegas, free to lose everything to the gamblers, sex slaves, and even weapons dealers who set up shop between the restaurants, gameshows, and travel bureaus.

So much money passed through the city's accounts and under its tables that the station was sometimes referred to as "The Laundry." Jules had thus far escaped being taken to the cleaners. Vegas *was* a fun place to visit. He just wished he could afford to live there.

He had changed his prints and the serial numbers on his eyes prior to coming to the spaceport to locate Crusher Cloud. It seemed quite possible to Jules that the trail was as cold as the backside of the Moon, but he had heard that the High Jinx casino was a good place to contact a dealer in stolen splat-lights.

Since the High Jinx was known for its Vision Duels, and Jules had a reputation under an assumed name as a winning duelist, he decided to create a scene to attract attention. This was not as foolish as it at first might seem, because, upon arriving at the crowded, noisy bar, his quarry had been pointed out to him, sitting in the back of the room at a small table, losing at micro-grav roulette. Nothing on Vegas gained a gambler's respect and interest better than a Vision Duel winner.

"The name's Xami Algiers," the man said, his dark hair hanging over one side of his face, shadowing his right eye. "And you're right, I'm interested in hiring your gaming skill."

Jules wanted to play this man carefully, like a trout on the line, to try and get the info he wanted without giving anything in return. "Terego," he said with a light smile. "Al Terego. Buy me a drink, Xami, and give me the score."

It seemed that Xami had recently experienced a significant unfortunate event. He nodded in the direction of a stunning blonde creature and explained, "I lost my personal data modules to him on a side bet."

Jules stretched his neck slightly to view the slot in the top of Xami Algiers's cranium. "Sort of picked your pocket, eh?"

Algiers took a pull on his drink. "I'm a sucker for a bluff and that guy could fool anybody."

"He certainly fooled me," Jules said, looking at the woman's chest.

"You don't know what it's like. I've got to have them back," Xami said, handing Jules a packet of playing chips. "Here's three thousand credits. You look like a man who can beat that guy's system."

This was better than Jules had hoped. He'd wanted to capture the man's attention by winning the duel, but it never occurred to him that he might also capture the man's trust. Now, if Jules didn't blow it, he had a good chance of having Xami in his debt. "All right, give me the three thousand. If I win, I get to keep it. If I lose, you walk away."

"Done," the man said, and Jules sensed a genuine feeling of gratitude.

"Stay here with your drink," Jules said. "I don't want to give away the fact that I'm playing for you. It might raise the stakes."

Algiers stayed at the bar, while Jules moved through the crowded room in the general direction of the roulette table. There were three other players losing big pots to the blonde. As he drew closer, Jules found it harder and harder to believe that this fellow hadn't been born female. He certainly looked it. He wondered fleetingly about the woman he'd kissed after winning his duel with the Italian.

"Excuse me," he said with his most smarming smile and fanned the three thousand credits in front of the transexual. "Could I perhaps see the 'lady' alone for a moment?"

The players looked up. A ruckus clanging from the back of the casino signaled that someone had hit it big at one of the slots. Jules caught the woman's eye.

She rested a hip against him. "The name's Odds," she said. "Even Steven Odds."

"Al Terego," he answered with a slight bow.

"Saw you in the Vision Duel, Al. What's your game?"

"Is there someplace less conspicuous where we can discuss it?" Jules answered, quickly adding: "Five minutes, promise."

The lady looked around the table. The other players seemed gratified for any excuse to delay their losses. Odds stood up. "Oh, what the hell? I need to take a whiz, anyway."

Jules followed her into the public accommodations. Minutes later, they parted ways—Jules with the pull-pouch of mods and the "woman" with ten thousand cred-its. Jules had decided not to leave anything to chance. He had purchased the mods, outright, intending to get the money back later, one way or another. There had been a brief discussion about laying odds, but Jules had gra-ciously begged off.

With a slight jerk of his head, he indicated that Xami was to meet him in the corridor. While waiting, Jules quickly applied a tiny bug to the outer casing of one of the data modules. When Xami came out of the High Jinx bar, the two men walked along together, avoiding the commercials that sang and flashed around and above them.

"You were lucky, partner." Jules casually handed Xami the pouch. "She's a sucker for video-reddog."

"That lousy trans—" Xami carefully looked through the bag's contents to be sure his possessions were all there.

Jules waved the three thousand in Xami's direction. "In fact, I won so much from her, there's no charge for the service."

"Hey," Xami said, "you keep it, partner. I always pay my debts."

Jules doubted this very much, but still insisted that the man take back his money. He didn't have to suggest it a third time.

"Listen," Xami said as they walked along, pushing away the thought balloons that tried to tease them into the clubs. "How'd you like to make some big money?"

*Easy*, Jules thought. *Don't let him know you're too interested.* "I don't know. Is it risky?"

"You could say that." Xami laughed. "But it shouldn't bother a quick and clever guy, like you."

Jules turned on the man, slamming him up against the wall, his right forearm pressing against Xami's throat, while the left quickly searched for weapons. Xami's eyes bulged, his mouth making a gagging sound. A small mechanical device bumped into Jules's leg, asking for spare change. Jules nudged it away as he found a heavy truncheon under the left arm of Xami's jacket.

"My, my," he said, backing away and inspecting the

club. "And I'll bet it produces a good 50,000 Volts when I press this button."

"You shit!" Xami cried, rubbing his throat with one hand and reaching for the baton with the other. "Give it back!"

"Whoa, partner," Jules said, holding the weapon away from its owner. "You know, if we're to work together, I need some assurance that you mean me no harm. I played your game. Now you play mine—without any surprises."

Xami continued to massage his neck, but he let his other hand drop. "All right. I guess that's fair, but if you ever jump me again, I'll—"

The begging droid came back, and Jules zapped it with a charge from the truncheon. The pestering device sputtered, shook, and then froze in its tracks. "Oops," Jules said and looked up to find Xami shaking his head in laughter.

"All right," the man said. "Follow me."

They took a few turns through the Vegas corridors, each time encountering fewer and fewer passers-by. Jules realized that the commercial crowds were thinning, because he and Xami were nearing the station's central police bureau. Nobody liked to buy, sell, or con around the headquarters of the stern and somewhat-elitist Vegas cops. The tourist felt secure, knowing that the Vegas police were there to protect them, but the locals had good reason to avoid authority whenever possible.

Jules wondered why Xami led him to a storage chamber so close to the police HQ.

Xami shut and sealed a door behind them and then opened a hatch in the room's floor. "Go ahead, Al," he said. "I thought you liked to gamble."

Jules stepped back, waving the baton. "After you, by all means."

Xami grunted and proceeded down the ladder.

Jules placed the weapon under his arm and followed the man down. The compartment below hummed with power. It appeared to be an access to the police station's utility hub, jammed full of communications panels, conduits and electrical switching grids. It was cramped, poorly-lighted and smelled of warm plastic and ozone.

As they reach the bottom of the ladder, Xami stepped back and smiled. "Who'd ever check to see if the cops were losing power? Nobody bothers us, because nobody likes coming down here."

Jules peered around the dusty, humming environment. "Surely, a maintenance crew comes through once in a while.

Xami laughed. "We are the maintenance crew."

"We?"

"Just wait," Xami responded, slipping one of his mods into the top of his head and typing a long sequence into a keyboard attached to a door. The seal broke and the door opened to expose another passageway beyond.

Jules followed Xami through. "I can't believe that no

one knows about this compartment when space in Vegas is at a premium."

Two wireheads approached, raising sharp pikes to recognize or bar Xami's entrance, but the man confidently waved them away. "Shadow's expecting me." Then he jerked a thumb at Jules. "And he's with me." The two guards went back to sucking on cruise current.

Xami walked into another compartment and called out, "Shadow?"

Jules followed, beginning to lose his bearings.

"Hey, Shadow, it's me! And, I think I've got just the guy for that heist we were talking about."

Jules looked around, but saw no one. He stayed close to Xami, suspecting some sort of ambush. The room was like a large hotel suite. There was an entertainment console, a bed, a toilet, a closet, two adjustable chairs and a game table. It was neat, clean and tidy. A large holo-screen filled one wall, but it was turned off now, not even displaying its ubiquitous ads.

Jules suspected that the mysterious Shadow-person might be in the toilet, or even the closet.

Xami fiddled with the entertainment console. "Well, I guess we'll just have to wait. How about a drink?"

One of the wirehead guards walked in behind them. Turning, Jules watched as it lifted its mask and peeled away the hook and loop seams of its holo-suit, stepping out to reveal itself as a dark, satin clad woman of unusual beauty. The skin of her cheeks and the backs of her hands was a bizarre mosaic of jeweled patterns. "Keep away from that," she ordered, moving regally past Jules without a glance. "You'll need your wits clear for tomorrow's assault."

"Okay, I'm impressed," Jules said. "Now, does the other one turn into the Amazing Warpman?"

The woman glanced at him, coolly. "Who's the freelance?"

Xami put his glass down, regretfully. "We need somebody with a rep for risk and gamble," he said, rubbing his throat again. "This guy won a tough Vision Duel and he got me out of an even tougher spot. He's clever and skilled and thinks he'd be perfect for getting us that jewel."

The woman almost hissed as she approached. *Must be the swish of her satin outfit*, Jules thought.

"Tough guy, huh?" Her green eyes flashed.

Jules smirked. "What's with all the silly dialogue? Xami said something about making big money, but you two are acting like a bad dramody."

The woman stepped back and again reached under her neck to peel away a second holo-suit.

Jules watched, mouth slightly open. "Okay. This time I'm really impressed."

The woman before him now was under 150 cm and must have weighed less than fifty kg. She the strangest eyes Jules had ever encountered. The pupils seemed dull and blank under her lids. Her hair was short, straight, and blonde. She was dressed in a black woolover work suit, and her skin was a pale as paste.

"No more games, Mr. Terego," she said, reaching for a key on the entertainment console. The wall screen glowed and Jules saw himself played back larger than life and a little dark due to Xami's drooping lock of hair. He heard his voice say, "If I win, I get to keep it. If I lose, you walk away." Then Xami's voice said, "Done," and the woman muted the sound.

"So, he's got a funny eye," Jules told them. "So what?"

"You're right, Xami." She walked back to stand beside him. "He's very quick. I think he'll do nicely."

Jules was starting to worry. Perhaps now would be a good time to use the Link and update the rest of Tripleye. Well, maybe a little bit more info was needed first. "Do nicely for what? And just who the hell are you, anyway?"

The woman pressed another key on the console. The view on the wallscreen changed to a near-range perspective of Spaceport Vegas with a surrounding cluster of supply and pleasure ships attending it. The combined albedo masked the stars beyond station, making it appear to be floating in solid blackness.

"This is the private cruiser, *Innsbruck,* owned by the head of the Volksfarbar Corp, Leo Fleischmann," the woman said as the view zoomed in to display one of the more ornate objects moving in the city's orbit. "Tomorrow, I propose to board the cruiser and retrieve an object which Volksfarbar stole from its rightful owners."

"That's grand theft," Jules said.

The woman ignored him. "The object is a data crystal, containing information about our Cause and the names of all our members. If I don't get it back, Volksfarbar will use it to persecute everyone who is against his corporation. Thousands, perhaps millions, of lives will be altered. To get it back, I cannot afford to employ anyone with a weak heart or mind. So, I had to tease you—just a little."

Jules watched as the screen presented a cut-away view of the orbiting ship. It was a professional job, so there was money in this somewhere, but none of this was info that had anything to do with why he'd come to Vegas.

"You keep speaking in the first person, and we've not been formally introduced," he said. "I know it would be rude, if I decided to leave now, especially since you've told me the beginning of your interesting story, so why not tell it all? Let's start with who you are."

The woman shut off the screen and stepped toward him, placing a palm on the side of his face. "You will know me only as Shadow Stone. I am a loyal member of Weave Corp."

*I love it*, Jules thought. Weave Corp was the company that had employed the thieves who'd stolen the weapons from Achilles, Mars.

Jules's deception had paid off. Crusher Cloud was

the chief bodyguard for Weave Corp's CEO, Eric Von Roon. The trail was hot again.

"Okay." Xami sounded uncomfortable interrupting. "Then the introductions are over, so I say we hit the ship tonight."

The shadow woman turned away from Jules's gaze. "No, we stay with the plan and do it in the morning. Besides, we haven't discussed Mr. Terego's fee." She turned back, almost smiling. "Would twenty-five thousand credits persuade you to help us get back the data crystal?"

Tempting as the offer sounded, money wasn't what Jules was after. Crusher had killed the Tripleye agency's youngest op, while escaping from Mars. Jules wanted to get back at the people who planned the robbery and committed the murder.

There were huge games being played by the Weave Corp, games that affected interplanetary trade and politics.

Forces were assembling for a major battle. He could feel it in his bones. And that meant this was a perfect place for a gambler named Jules St. Mathew.

He looked again at the woman's strange eyes. "Shadow," he said, "you've just hired yourself a thief."

↝↜

"Do you think he suspects?" Xami's voice intoned.

"Possibly," the woman answered. "A man like Terego thrives on high adventure and higher risk."

Jules was listening to them over the micro-transmission of his planted bug. They had given him a small room with comfortable furnishings and a carafe of wine which he promptly poured down the toilet drain. A brief scan of his surroundings assured him that he was not being electronically observed, so he had decided to take the initiative by listening in on his hosts' conversation.

Xami's voice continued. "Maybe we should send a vax to Von Roon, just to make sure he has a solid alibi for the time of our raid?"

Shadow sighed. "Von Roon is a—" She stopped herself. "He's nearing the Moon, by now. I'm sure he's arranged for suitable protection."

The plan as generally outlined by Shadow called for Xami, Jules, and herself to enter the Volksfarbar cruiser, disguised as Vegas safety inspectors. Then they would split up, each keeping a portion of the ship's crew occupied, while Jules stole the data crystal. The safety inspection equipment came housed in a small tool box, which was where Jules would secret the jewel, prior to the team's exit.

Shadow had shown him a replica of the treasure—an oddly-faceted, rainbow-streaked gem the size of an eyeball, kept secure in a stasis field in the vessel's executive conference room. The prize was thrilling and the task challenging, but Jules was suspicious of the players in this caper. These were very tricky people. He decided to minimize his risk by making an effort to Link to the agency. '*Chico, darling,*' he said, stiffening. '*It's me.*'

'*Hi, me,*' the Korean woman responded. '*What's happening on Vegas?*'

Jules was disappointed. '*You sound strange. Is something wrong?*'

'*No—yes. It's this damn audit. Doc's got me working nearly three shifts, digging out old tax records, as well as running Link Central. If you've got an update, let's have it. I'm buried in work.*'

Quickly, Jules passed her the latest info on Weave Corp and Von Roon. '*There's a chance that the stolen goods and Crusher Cloud are now with the Weave CEO on the Moon. I'll let you know for sure later.*'

His nerves started to signal intense pain. The stiffness was wearing on him more than usual, due to the vast distance his thoughts had to travel.

'*Jules?*'

'*Yes?*'

'*You sound funny. I think there's something wrong about the Link.*'

So, she sensed it too. '*See what you can find out about a stolen data cube,*' he said. '*Weave wants it back real bad. Can you hear me all right?*'

'*Just barely. I'll tell Doc what you said. Be careful, and don't run up the expense account. Remember, we're fighting for the life of the agency.*'

'*Yes, Mother. I'll be good.*'

She snickered and was gone from his mind.

After his nerves and muscles loosened, Jules switched the bug on again and listened.

"…I just checked on him," Xami was saying. "The wine worked beautifully! He's out cold, sleeping like a baby. But I locked the door, anyway."

*So the man checked on me while I was frozen under the side-effect of the Link? Good thing I decided to lie on the bed to do it.*

"Good," the woman answered. "We, too, should get some rest. We'll need all our strength tomorrow."

"It's funny," Xami said, "I'm not tired at all."

"Then you can play with your mods. I'm going to sleep."

Jules chuckled quietly.

೮ೞ೮ೞ

The "raid" seemed more like a casual outing. Jules was impressed at how well prepared his two companions were when undertaking of such a risky endeavor. They had already processed the necessary reports and credentials to allow access to the *Innsbruck*, and they had picked a time when the majority of its crew were off-ship, or otherwise engaged in a series of engine overhauls.

The *Innsbruck* was not a military vessel. It was a

pleasure ship on a sexcrusion cruise, currently stationed only three hundred meters beyond the spaceport's outer surface. Its passengers had come to Vegas to enjoy themselves and ostensibly conduct a few "liaison" meetings between various corps in the Innerplanetary System. Jules was astonished to find several priceless works of art on board, none of which were small enough to be secreted away under the current circumstances, unfortunately.

While Xami and Shadow Stone went forward to file reports that would further occupy the ship's passengers and crew, Jules made a direct line for the stasis field hidden inside a holo-console in the ship's main conference room, while wondering about his "safety." Before leaving Vegas, Xami had checked the function of his stun baton and Shadow Stone had demonstrated a remarkable skill with a nunchaku, the close-order combat weapon made popular during the Belt War. Jules had never cared for the things, but he had to admit that she spun the solid sections of black tubing around on their chains in a series of blurring arcs that looked impressively lethal.

For his part, Jules had selected a keen-edged, silvery rapier from Shadow's stock of interesting armaments, but there was no way he could have disguised the weapon enough to smuggle it aboard the *Innsbruck*. Xami quickly pointed out that this didn't matter, since their job was to protect him and his job to steal the jewel. Still, Jules was uncomfortable with the arrangement and hurried to complete his task ahead of schedule, while occasionally eavesdropping, via the bugged mod, on his companions and their hypothetical emergency drills.

He concentrated the majority of his attention on the task at hand. Even under normal circumstances, nullifying a stasis field was not easy. Within the solid black block, time had virtually stopped. Things were frozen and protected from the effects of normal kinetic decay. If the crystal cube were in there, nothing could get it out while the field was operative. The field, originally, appeared to have been inserted only into the holo-unit, but a closer inspection proved that it was actually lodged in the ship's hull. That meant it couldn't be removed without damaging the airtight integrity and setting off alarms. But it could be turned off, if you knew the proper code to insert into the lock's computer.

Under the guise of safety inspections, it was acceptable for Jules and the others to cause short disruptions along the power grid as they made their rounds throughout the ship. Within the first few minutes, Jules had located three separate power lines, one of which had to be the supply for the field and its control unit. He extracted a small device from his tool box that looked like ordinary Ohm-meter and attached it to the field's control. Prior to boarding the pleasure craft, Xami had demonstrated a special use for the item which tricked the control into thinking it was still receiving power from its normal source, instead of a backup battery. Thus defeated, the alarm signal which should have pulsed out when the main power was interrupted or never issued from the field's controller.

After making a few rapid adjustments to the bogus tester, St. Mathew cut the power on the first line and was delighted to think that he'd made the correct choice first try out of three.

Then he realized that the air in the compartment was no longer circulating and the field was still solid. *Oh well, no harm done, just go on to the other two lines*. He re-connected the first line and shut off the second. Immediately, the room plunged into total blackness. *Not to worry. Not to worry*.

He had a pocket flash in the tool box. Switching it on, Jules saw that the field was still stubbornly intact.

While the darkness surrounded him, Jules had the eerie sensation that someone was watching him, or rather that he was watching someone else. It felt a bit like the Link, except that he wasn't frozen. Nevertheless, there was a strong inclination that Shadow was nearby and speaking. No, not speaking—thinking.

Jules reconnected the line and the sensation went away. As an experiment, he darkened the room again and was certain that he heard the woman reviewing in her mind the ambush that was planned for St. Mathew as soon as he finished stealing the crystal.

*I can't be hearing this*, Jules thought. *I'm not using the Link and Shadow isn't even conditioned for it. Or, is she?* Could some people naturally be able to tap into the

Link? Did the woman know that her thoughts were being driven? The sound seemed very faint. *If I let my concentration waver, it vanishes.*

Jules turned on the lights and tried to focus his mind by closing his eyes. Yes, he was getting it again. Shadow and Xami had planned to kill him and leave his body as a scapegoat for the crime. But the woman was wishing she could ambush Xami, instead of Jules. Unfortunately, Xami had been appointed to assist her by Chancellor Von Roon, himself, so by default, Jules was the one who would have to go.

Jules opened his eyes and set himself the task of simultaneously shutting down the second and third power line. Instantly, he was back in the blackness, but he kept his mind on his work. The pocket flash showed that, this time, the field had dissolved, exposing not only the cube, but also a packet of gambling chips and miniature stun gun.

In the darkness, Jules uttered a single word which summed up his feelings and signaled a threat to his ungodly companions. The phrase was "Gotcha."

Minutes later, he was out of the compartment with his prize tucked away in a pocket and the stun gun hidden in his hand. Shadow was the first to arrive at the exit port, and Jules confronted her with the weapon.

She was wearing her ornately jeweled disguise, but it didn't hide the surprise in her eyes. Her pretty little mouth demanded, "What are you doing?"

Jules kept his distance, knowing that the stun gun's range was longer than the woman's nunchaku.

"Let's call it insurance, darling," he said. "I've got the jewel and I think perhaps we should leave now, together."

Before she could answer, Xami came around a corner in the passageway, holding his stun baton at the neck of a hostage. "I found her in the room, playing licking games with Fleischmann. Could've killed her too, but a hostage might—" He stopped.

"Well, well, well," Jules concentrated on keeping his voice and his aim steady. "So, now it's murder. I suspected some sort of secondary purpose for this grand excursion, but I didn't expect to meet you again."

Xami's hostage was the shapely he/she gambler, Even Steven Odds, from the High Jinx bar.

⁌⁍

Had he been a more callus and less adventuresome soul, Jules might have stunned them all and escaped with the boodle. But that would have ended his lead to Crusher and Von Roon. As it stood, Jules decided that an extended bluff might be the more profitable response, since he was now dealing with an assassin.

"Okay, kids," he said. "We're all still partners in the same old dance. It's just my turn to lead. Let's get out of here, before someone discovers our handiwork." He gestured to the exit with the stun gun and Xami looked at Shadow questioningly. The woman moved through the exit without a word and Xami followed with his hostage.

The journey back through Vegas was eventful, in that each person attempted to ask a question, only to be cautioned to shut up by another. The city's corridors were still busy with advertisements and pitchmen. Jules could hardly control his little band, as they made their way through the crowd of pulse-skating tourists and casino employees.

Jules would have liked to Link to Chico back on Mars, but he knew it would stiffen his muscles and leave him helpless. He decided to continue his confidence strategy and try to gain more info on Crusher and Von Roon. Barring that, he could always fall back on stunning his companions and searching their quarters for a lead to Weave Corp.

"Hey, Terego," Xami said, just before the group arrived at the secret entrance near the police station. "I don't want this guy to know any more about our operation than absolutely necessary."

"Let me go," Odds said. "I won't say anything to anyone anyway."

"Sure, you won't." Xami nodded. "A little tap with my truncheon will put you to sleep for as long as I like. What do you say, Terego."

Jules looked at Shadow. Perhaps he could use the situation to strengthen his position with these terrorists.

"Set it for a mild stun," he said. "Enough to put her out so she doesn't see the entrance to our hideout. And, since was your idea, Xami, you can carry her."

Even Steven Odds glared at Jules when the stunner touched her head. "I'll get you for th—"

Her eyes rolled up as her body went slack. Jules tried to convince himself that in the long run she would be safer that way.

"Now, Mr. Terego," Shadow said, once they'd all passed through the power station and arrived at the hideout, "what is the meaning of this effrontery? Did you think that we would not pay you?"

Xami put the he/she on a cushioned floater, where it began to snore.

"Oh, I knew you'd pay me," he answered, keeping his weapon directed at the two of them. "I just wanted to make sure that it was in the right kind of currency."

The woman's glare was fire-like. "Is that supposed to be funny?"

"Yeah," Xami added. "I warned you once. I don't like having guns pointed at me."

"And I don't like surprises, remember?" Jules replied. "Put your weapons on the floor and kick them to me."

The two baton-like devices clattered on the hard deck and slid to where Jules stood. He picked them up and tucked one under each arm. "Okay, I want some answers. Why did you kill Fleischmann?"

Shadow casually sat in a chair, bold as hell. "He was a fool. Worse than that, he was a powerful fool. The chancellor offered him a ranking position in the Neo-Socialist Order. He would have been the number two man, but he refused."

"By the chancellor, you mean Von Roon, right?"

Her glare became seemingly hotter, if that was possible. "He is the greatest political force on Earth. The names on the cube you've stolen will help us consolidate our forces and root out any detractors. We'll be free to go forward to the New Order."

"I knew you weren't telling me everything," Jules said, shaking his head, "but are you talking about Nazis?"

"*Naturlich*," the woman said. "Do you doubt that we will be a force to be reckoned with?"

"Not when you talk like that," Jules answered. "Listen, I'm all for playing politics, but you were planning on double crossing me."

Xami seemed to be holding his breath.

Jules played his trump. "Under the circumstances, I think that's worth a bonus, don't you?"

Xami relaxed, smiling. "I told you this guy was good."

The woman rose from her chair, accepting the bait. "No, Xami. All he cares about is money. Come, Mr. Terego. Your credits are in another room."

"Uh, what about Xami and his little friend here?"

The woman sighed. "They'll be no problem. I will lock them in, while we get your pay."

Jules certainly appreciated the benefits of money, but right now he was still more interested in securing information.

He suspected that the woman might act differently toward him once she was away from Xami. After all, they had yet to be alone together for more than a few seconds, and this strange, unemotional beauty intrigued him.

"I've got a better idea," Jules said and fired a short blast from the stunner. Xami fell next to his hostage. Soon the room was filled with stereo snoring.

Upon entering the next room, Shadow unlocked a small status field and begrudgingly paid out the twenty-five thousand credits, plus a ten-thousand credit bonus.

Jules accepted the payment with a smile and decided the time was right to probe for more information. "Do you know how I knew about the ambush, back on the *Innsbruck?*"

The woman's eyes flashed hard enough to cut plex. "You interfered somehow with my mind."

"So you felt it, too, eh? You know, Xami's not the kind of second-in-command that you need on an operation of this sort. I am."

The woman looked away. "Xami's a fool, but he's loyal to the Cause."

"He's a bigger fool than you think," Jules said, pressing home his advantage. He had to get beyond this woman's defenses. "Here, let me show you." He reached into his belt pouch and turned on the receiver connected to the bug.

Xami was awake and talking to Odds. "You mean he bought my mods back from you? He said he won them."

"Hell, no," the trans said. "Nobody beats me at reddog. Now I've helped you and told you the truth. How about letting me go?"

Jules started to switch off the sound.

"Very resourceful, Mr. St. Mathew. But how stupid do you think I am?" She had meant to shock him by using his correct name, but Jules was not surprised. She had used the name previously in her thoughts aboard the pleasure ship, when she was regretting the ambush. Now there was absolutely no trace of regret in her tone or stony features. "I'm tired of these silly games! I ran a background check on you last night, and learned you are an agent of a small investigations company on Mars."

"Intensive Investigations, Incorporated," Jules said. "We like to call ourselves Tripleye, and our corporation may be small in comparison—"

"What does it matter, Mr. St. Mathew--"

"Call me Jules."

Finally, there was a faint spark of emotion in her eyes. She raised her hand in a strange gesture.

Jules heard a sound behind him and turned to see that the woman had signaled one of the wirehead who guarded the door. The big man lunged at him with his long, sharp pike.

☙❧

Jules dodged the attack and attempted a spin kick that came off rather clumsily, considering the number of items he was holding. His stun gun went skidding across the room. The move had placed him in a prime location to zap the brute with Xami's baton, but the wirehead took the charge and enjoyed it!

Saliva ran from the corners of the giant's grinning mouth as he swung at Jules.

Jules back-pedaled away, realizing he had lost track of Shadow. The wirehead advanced, and Jules switched his defense to the nunchaku still under his arm. He was not proficient with the weapon, but he figured all he needed was one lucky blow to the big man's head. Instead, he nearly cracked the knuckles of his own left hand, while awkwardly attempting to spin the damn things in his attacker's face. *This is ridiculous*, he thought, ducking under the wirehead's arms.

Coming up from behind, Jules quickly jumped upon the man's broad back, twisting the chain of the nunchaku around his opponent's throat. He pulled tight, with all of his strength, restricting the brute's windpipe. The man tried unsuccessfully to slam Jules against the wall. Together, they tumbled into another room, the giant showing the first signs of weakening.

Jules held on as the wirehead bucked and tried to tear him free. After a few seconds, Jules jumped back and clubbed the big man unconscious with a convenient chair.

Looking around, he saw that they were in the weapons room. Thank God for that! Shadow Stone and his missing stun gun were gone, but his spirits rose as he located the polished rapier he had eyed earlier. His hand felt comfortable on the hilt, and he wasted no time dashing back to the room where he'd left Xami and the trans.

They were still there. Xami had gotten back his baton and was holding at the he/she's neck.

"Get out of my way," he warned, seeing the sword in Jules hand.

Jules glanced around the room. No sign of Shadow. "Give it up, Xami. Release the—whatever."

Xami laughed. "Forget it!"

Jules decided to try a bluff. "I put a program virus on one of your mods," he said, and Xami's eyes grew wild. "If you leave now, you'll never be able to stop it from destroying all your precious data."

"Get me out of here!" the hostage said.

"Shut up," Xami growled, as he clumsily got out his mods and tumbled them onto a desktop.

"There." Jules moved forward, indicating the mod he had bugged.

Xami gave a deep-throated growl when he spotted the implanted circuit.

Jules seized the moment and kicked out a leg, throwing the man off balance. Jules quickly pulled the trans to him, but Xami's attention stayed on the mod.

There was something wrong here.

The hostage tried to pull away, but Jules caught the edge of a hook and loop seam and the holo-suit parted to expose Shadow's furious features. She'd been playing the part of the hostage and he had fallen for it. Hook, line, and sinker.

The woman clutched Jules's sword arm, pulling him down and throwing him against the entertainment console. Instantly, the wall screen sprang to life, flooding the room with flashes of light and color and the booming sound of several overlapping commercials.

Xami dashed forward with his stun baton, while the room seemed to fill with an ad for exotic food at your friendly, nearby McCoke. Jules retrieved his rapier, knowing he had the advantage of reach over the stubby truncheon.

*But where is the he/she? And now I lost Shadow, again.*

Then Xami did something that demanded immediate attention. Twisting the base of his stunner/truncheon, he shot the tip out in a spring-loaded sweep that extended his weapon to a length that matched St. Mathew's sword.

"Now, partner," he mocked, advancing with determination, his dark hair hanging over his eyes. "Let's see how good a fencer you are against 50,000 Volts!"

Jules caught the first blast just as an ad for disposable hair came smash-cutting across the wall behind them. "Be mean, be lean," it shouted. "Get all the sex you've ever seen!" And Xami hit him again with a hard jolt as their weapons crossed and sparked.

The pain was like nothing he had ever encountered. Each thrust and parry brought a new charge of stunning power up his arm and into his brain.

"Fantasy salve!" the wall announced. "It burns where you yearn."

Jules staggered and spun away, dodging another zapping stroke from Xami's weapon. There was little escape, as the man pressed his advantage, following him out the door and into the dusty utility hub. The second he heard the humming of the police station's circuits, Jules thought desperately of the missing stun gun. And, then Xami hit him again with a glancing charge of electrical energy.

"So you wanted to take over my job?" the man growled.

"Wait," Jules cried, fumbling in his belt pouch. "I've still got the crystal. I'll give it to you!"

"You'll give it to me, all right. And anything else you've got." To emphasize his point, Xami pressed the tip of his truncheon directly against St. Mathew's shoulder. Immediately, the arm went numb and the sword clattered to the deck.

Hoping to distract his attacker, Jules used his functioning hand to pitch the object across the passage to the floor next to a switching unit. The humming sound seemed to be inside him now, surging up his spine in a way that was ten times stronger than the Link. He dropped to the deck.

Xami pulled back to watch him suffer. "This beats a Vision Duel all to hell, doesn't it?" He laughed, strolled to the switching unit, and stooped to grasp his prize.

Jules hefted the rapier like a spear, hoping to pin his opponent against the wall.

Xami saw it coming. He knocked the sword to one side with a wide sweep of his truncheon that caught between two power leads, trapping his body in an enormous electrical circuit. There was a bright white flare and a howling scream, and then the lights went out.

Jules was doubly blinded, once by the flash on his retinas and again by the darkness around him. The residual effects of Xami's weapon were filling Jules with a cacophony of disorienting impulses. He thought he could hear Shadow, but the sound was faint. He didn't know if it was actual or the Link.

*And I don't really care*, he thought, as he came unsteadily to his feet. *I can't tell for sure what's real and what isn't. She still wants the cube, but she wants to escape even more and she can still use the trans as a hostage.*

The emergency lights flared on in small amber pools throughout the passageway.

'*Shadow*,' he linked. '*Can you hear me?*'

There was no direct answer, only a general feeling of panic.

'*Yes, you hear me,*' Jules continued, fumbling his way to the door. '*I told you that you needed a new second-in-command.*' He glanced at the fused and steaming remains of Xami Algiers, whose tissue seemed to glisten and glow with each surge of power. The smell was hideous. '*Xami's gone and so's the crystal cube. It's just you and me now.*'

'*How are you doing this?*' the woman answered. '*Get out of my head!*'

'*I'm not only in your head,*' Jules said, stretching the point. '*I'm also in contact with the police. They'll be down here in a few minutes to clean up the remains of your hideout and take you into custody.*'

'*Don't come any nearer, or I will kill the girl.*'

Jules stumbled forward. The Link seemed weak again. Its strength seemed in inverse proportion to Jules's. '*Come now, darling. Don't we have enough bodies lying around already?*'

'*There!*' she linked, in triumph. '*It is done.*'

'*What? What done?*'

The woman's thoughts were growing fainter. '*I've injected a poison into the trans. She will die in seconds, while I escape.*'

Jules discovered new strength and rushed into the main room to find the he/she crudely bound and in a chair. A quick and unpleasant inspection proved that the hostage was not wearing a holo-suit.

Jules felt his muscles tightened as he received a faint Link. '*This is not the end, St. Mathew. We are bigger than you think. I promise you, Tripleye will feel our full power soon. Within a month.*'

Jules pulled a gag from the he/she's mouth, hoping he was in time to save her.

"Hurry," Odds coughed. "She went a door behind that wall screen!"

Jules stepped back and glanced in the indicated direction. "But—"

"But nothing, buster. I'm okay. There wasn't any poison, fool. She bluffed you!"

In the space of the last few minutes, Jules had been stunned by Xami and frozen by the Link, but the news that he had been out-maneuvered by Shadow's latest deception affected him like a combination of the other two.

"Some big-time gambler you are," the transexual said.

Jules rushed to locate the hidden door, but it was sealed, of course. He knew he'd never get it open in time to catch her. She had escaped him with a grand bluff, and there was nothing else to do, except accept it and escape with the trans before the police arrived.

∾∾

"Okay," Odds said, coming over to sit at Jules table

to share a drink. "I've laundered your credits and gotten you booked on the Mars Shuttle. You're registered as a Mr. Mark Lukejohn. Umm…what kind of name is that?"

Jules put up a finger to hush her. "Careful." He glanced carefully around the High Jinx casino to ensure that none of the other partiers or players had heard the slip. "Unlike everyone else on this station, I don't want to advertise.

Odds shrugged. "Whatever you say, Mr. Terego." She handed the tickets and phony passport under the table. "I owe you for saving my dirty hide, so it's all on the house."

Jules ordered another drink. He had never been so totally bluffed before. In one way or another, he had always felt that he was truly superior to everyone he went up against. But now he'd been bested and possibly met his match.

Shadow Stone. What an unusual name. Who was she, really? And why had he sensed a strange deadness in her eyes? Obviously, she was in full control of her actions, yet Jules sensed there was something hovering over her, influencing her.

He tried again to Link to her, but there was no response. How could she be connected to the Link? And how had she learned so much about him so quickly? From now on, he would have to be constantly on his guard. And yet, he looked forward to meeting her again.

As the shuttle left Vegas on its flight back to Achilles, Jules gazed out the porthole at the dwindling spaceport, home of high living, high adventure, and higher risk. He fingered the data crystal hidden in his pocket. "You were right, Xami. Sometimes we're all suckers for a bluff."

# CHAPTER 4

## *THE AXIS EX-PATRIOT*

I can handle this," Pat said with resolve and conviction. It was an outward attempt to deal with her intensive pain and churning stomach.

The peptide scrubbers finished circulating through her body, as they had for seven hours each day of the last two weeks. Ten more days of this fierce treatment, and she would be free of the radiation absorbed while shutting down the reactor at Achilles's sabotaged geo-therm plant. If the power center had reached meltdown, one of the most populous spots on Mars would have been uninhabitable for decades to come.

Pat gritted her teeth as another wave of pain shook her body. Because of her heroic actions, she now suffered through this therapy, slept to regain her strength, and watched the holo she'd received from Duke Lexington and his crew at the plant for "saving all our asses." She hated convalescing. There was too much work to be done at both of her businesses.

Someone knocked at the door of her private hospital room. "Hey, Doc, it's Wolf. The nurse said you were awake, but are you decent?"

The pain was fading and Pat managed to laugh a little. "Come on in, Wolf. I'm so desperate for something to take my mind off my condition, I'll even talk to you."

The husky man came into the room, his hat held in one hand and a portable Vax in the other. "Wait 'til you see what I brought you. This guy is sure to take your mind off your troubles," the bald operative said cheerily, placing the Vax on a wheeled table by the bed. He turned the display so that it faced Pat's pillowed head. "This guy is a genuine looney!"

Pat's other business was psychiatry. When she wasn't running the detective agency, she helped people adjust to the life around them. The two companies had a lot more in common than most people thought.

"Speaking of loonies," she kidded, "have you heard any more from your mysterious voices?"

The old op put his hat on, covering the slit at the top of his head where he loaded his data modules when accessing info on a case. The movement of his arm masked his features. "No. I only hear my mods and the rest of the ops when they're on the Link. Speaking of which—" He fumbled in a pocket of his jacket and brought out three small squibs. "—I brought you a few temporary doses." He looked around suspiciously. "In case you get lonely and want to talk to somebody."

Pat took the plastic tubes, enclosing them gingerly between her palms. "Thanks, Wolf. That was thoughtful, but I can't use them here. It might interfere with my treatment."

He looked at her with narrowing eyes.

"Believe me. It's not my viralphobia talking," she protested, "I'm over that now, and I've learned my lesson: teamwork counts. I'm working on overcoming my fears and staying connected to the other ops."

He still seemed skeptical.

"It's boring as hell in here, okay? I'd love to chat telepathically with you all. But the doctors say the radiation scrubbing is a severe drain on my bio-chemistry. A virus as complex as the Link might be too much strain on my system, right now."

"Okay," he said, "I believe you. And I understand about it being boring in here. I'm just about ready to doze off myself. That's why I brought you this." He held up a data chip and began inserting it into the Vax. "This looney came into the office the other day and started telling me that we were all in for terrible trouble. I wasn't sure if he was one of your psychiatric patients, or a client for the agency, or what. I'm still not sure."

There was a hesitant knock at the door and Chico

Kim shouldered her way in, loaded down with data files and printpads. Chico was one of the few Koreans in Achilles. Most of the others of her people preferred to live in the clans near Middle Spot, or work in the Belt, mining metals. Pat had met Chico on Ceres, years ago during the war, when they were both involved in a military operation. Chico had first used the Link then to help rescue its discoverer trapped in a bombed-out cavern deep in the asteroid. Pat observed the virus's telepathic effects and immediately saw potential for psychiatric treatment. When the war ended, the two women moved to the Martian boomtown of Achilles to test the Link's ability for long-range transmission.

Wolf stepped over to assist the short, black-haired Korean woman. "Hi, doll," he said, taking the bulk of her load. "I didn't know you were coming down here. This will work out better than I expected."

"Hi, Wolfy. Hi, Doc. I brought the files you wanted. Sorry that I'm a bit late. That audit put me way behind."

"I know," Pat said. "That's why I wanted to work on them while I was laid up here."

"Yeah, but Doc—" Wolf interrupted. "I'm telling you, you've got to take a look at this guy. He says he used to be the boss of Weave Corp."

Both women spoke at once. "What?"

"Yeah," Wolf continued, "he came in the other day, acting very weird and saying that he had to talk to you about the revenge Weave Corp and Von Roon are planning against Tripleye and the rest of Mars. Since he acted so strange, I figured he was nuts. Here, let me show you." He clicked-on the Vax and its display presented a head and shoulder shot of a handsome young man who shook with a constant rapid tremor.

Chico came around to the side of Pat's bed in order to view it more carefully. "What's wrong with him?"

"He'll tell you in a minute," Wolf said. "I had him record this statement, rather than take the risk of bringing him down here. Maybe I'm a little paranoid, but you don't need any attacks on your life, now that you're such a big hero."

"You mean, now that she's so sick," Chico said.

Pat ignored both of them. "Where is this man now?"

"I've got him out cold in my apartment."

Pat raised an eyebrow. "Out cold?"

"Well…"

"You'd better get back there. Chico and I have a lot to do, but we'll be sure to study this. Back it up. I want to see it again from the beginning."

"I've got more files to bring in, Doc," Chico said. "I can sort them while we watch."

Wolf came around to give Chico a light squeeze. "Need any help carrying them?"

"Sure, Wolfy. That would be nice."

"A man's gotta do what a man's gotta—" Wolf said as they left together.

"Hey, you two!" Pat called. "Wheel this thing over

where I can reach it, before you go wandering off into the sunset."

Wolf complied, gesturing at the display with his thumb. "Have Chico link to me, if you need any further info on this character. I'll ask the questions for you and link back the answers through her."

Pat nodded, turning back to the Vax as her two employees left the room.

～∾～

"My name is Maxwell Jannings. You've probably heard of my father, Robert Jannings, the past president and CEO of Weave Corp. By regulation, I was briefly his successor, after his death. The Jannings tradition stretches back almost two centuries to the late twentieth, when East and West Germany were finally united as part of the spirit of glasnost. Under the circumstances, I had a pretty good life, growing up the heir of the globe's largest and most productive corp, but that was a lot of years ago.

"I know I appear young and healthy to you, except for this damn trembling syndrome, but everything you see here is the effect of a rather expensive drug I began taking nearly twenty-five years ago. Of course, it was first given to me by that bastard, Von Roon.

"Eric Von Roon is what I've come to warn you about. He is the most influential and possessive man on Earth. I know because for years he possessed me.

"I understand from the news reports that you've had moderate success in stopping him. My congratulations on that, and I hope we can pool our resources and have similar success on Earth. To understand the terrible depths of the man, you must see what he has done to me, my father, and the entire globe. Believe me, he is monstrously insane!"

⌘⌘⌘

Pat pushed a key on the Vax and began transcribing her impressions into the machine's resident memory.

"Subject Maxwell Jannings displays an almost melodramatic attitude. This could be based on fear, conviction or skilled acting. Minor indications of artistic background in syntax and word choice. Subject's physical affliction appears similar to untreated rheumatism or chorea. This is a fascinating 'confession.' There is an alluring temptation about his message. Even when I employ my most analytical posture, I find I'm drawn to learn more."

She turned the Vax on again.

⌘⌘⌘

"I've been instructed by Mr. Archerson to explain myself fully and completely from the beginning. I assume this is because you can't ask questions of a recording. I'd prefer to speak to you directly, but he has explained your circumstances, so I must be content with this clumsy method of communication.

"I was born ln 2044 in Prague, the capital city of Czech Republic. My father was an executive of a German oil company, working off the shores of Ethiopia in the Red Sea. These are all Earth locations, of course.

"His offices were just outside the ancient twin cities of Asmara and Massawa. I remember visiting him there with my mother when I was very young. He took us out in a small boat to one of the company's huge, off-shore derricks. It was hot, noisy and smelled of raw petro. I was glad to return to our estate in Prague, where life was comfortable and quiet, surrounded by my many tutors and servants.

"If you could have visited Prague before the Plutonium Leakage of 2063, you would have seen one of the most beautiful cities in all of the world. Our heritage goes back a millennia, something you Martians probably find disturbing. Ah, but the Neo-Europeans enjoyed wonders that you will have to wait centuries to experience. Warm traditions, ancient cultural influences, a history that lives on and on, even today all over the globe, due to the strength and flourishment of our essential corporate structure. You see, I don't blame the basic corpolitial system for Earth's many ills, only its current despotic leader.

"Would you believe that when I was a child in old Prague a woman still came past our city house every twilight to light the gas lamps along our street? The old traditions never die. One lamp was right outside my first-story window, and I could see her drifting out of the dusk along the cobblestones with her little dog and her ten-foot pole with its flame at the tip. She would lift her pole as if in salute to me and its little hook would catch the lamp's glass door, swing it back with a tiny creak, and the flame would enter the lamp like a hummingbird's beak into the heart of a flower.

"For a moment, our faces were suffused with the glow and she would smile up at me where I pressed against the fogging window. Then she would move off through the falling snow, leaving me with her warm and protective light. I never knew her name, nor do I know what ever became of her, but she often returns in my memory as an example of the wonderful heritage we Earth people offer the rest of mankind.

"Unfortunately, we also have our dark moments as well. Many of you Martians claim that we are tainted by our past, that we carry within us the failures and misspent opportunities of mankind's rise. When I was younger, I thought this was all propagandist nonsense, but now I know that there is something to what you say. Von Roon has shown me that the old ways die hardest when they are tinged with despotism. But you won't understand the significance of this, until you've heard me out.

"Did I say I was a poet? Well, I wanted to be one once. As a young man, I shunned the responsibilities of my position in my father's business. And when my sister

Marie was born, my mother's attention was drawn to her, so I began to find interest in the Arts.

"I discovered the world of the library. A place that at first seemed enormous and incomprehensible. Yet later, as I found my way through the shelves and stacks of fiction and the textbooks of half-recalled truth, the library became a comforting and familiar—almost secret—place for me. I imagined that it had been built by all the saints and scholars of the past, in order to pass on their hard-earned knowledge, so that I might piece reality together in some new and important way and change or evolve human awareness to its next level of development.

"I—I'm trying to explain my feelings about this, because I understand that you are a psychiatrist. By now, I'm sure you have formed an opinion about my way of expressing myself. Part of my trouble is, of course, the drug I mentioned earlier.

"Over the years, it has weakened my determination, until I am only motivated to act by the strongest of all emotions—fear. But I've come to believe that there are other influences on my life and that some of them originate from that mysterious and beautiful city where I was born. I can never go back there, but as Franz Kafka, another more-famous native of the old Czechoslovakian capitol, one wrote, 'Prague won't let go. This dear mother has claws.'"

❧❦❧

Doc Pat turned off the Vax and amended her audio notes.

"This is a very disturbed individual. I can see now why Wolf brought me this recording, rather than the man himself. I can also see why he wisely arranged to keep the man away from me while I'm on the mend. Maxwell Jannings is so unbalanced that I'm afraid he could become dangerous at any moment. He requires confinement and dependency treatment, but his problems will not be completely resolved until he overcomes his paranoid and nostalgic tendencies.

"I still do not yet understand the point of his confession/appeal. A link through Chico and Wolf would provide an opportunity for dialogue and cross-questioning. I will continue to review the program until Chico's return. Her perceptions might even lend new insight to this patient's unusual condition."

Pat keyed the Vax back to display mode.

ҪҪ

"Kafka was a strong influence on me during my early years as a poet. There is something almost mystical about his work. Something hauntingly real about his fantasies. And yet, they live on. There is a legend that Kafka's ghost inhabited the clock tower of the old town hall in Prague. This enormous fifteenth-century horologe was covered with small statuettes of rats, demons and winged monkeys, a fitting place for a ghost story, don't you think?

"The clock displayed not only the time, but the signs of the ancient Zodiac. Its huge face was flanked by the figures of Death, Invaders, Vanity, and Miserliness. The vision of this clock was so wonderful that the town fathers blinded its maker so that no other city would ever have a clock so fine.

"No, I don't believe the story. Nor do I believe that Kafka haunts the town, not literally. But the power of his prose is so strong that such stories are believed by millions of New-Europeans, and it is just that sort of weak, hopeful thinking that makes the majority of mankind open to the suggestions of a skilled and powerful orator/executive like Von Roon.

"Perhaps now you are beginning to see the strength of this man. There is something majestic about him, something that appeals to the Earth people with all their centuries of conqueror heritage. He almost knows what you're thinking before you think it. A sort of pre-cog telepath, who has enhanced his position with the common man, until he totally dominates the masses with his artful diplomacy and promises of a glorious future.

"I realize what I am saying seems insolent and demented. You probably suspect that the flaw is within me, rather than the corpolitical leader of a planet. So let me explain what I know of Von Roon's history. Then you can see, in context, the terrible threat of his famous Banners Victory speech. Just understand for now that the man has a way of getting more than a person's full attention. When I was under his influence, I never held back a gram! I attacked problems he gave me head on, never flinching or doubting, and that sort of attitude is untroubled, confident, and almost addictive in itself to anyone who feels oppressed, over-worked, or put upon by the circumstances or station in their life.

"I first met Eric Von Roon in the winter of 2072, when he carne to our estate accompanying my sister who was returning on Christmas vacation from Leipzig University. We had moved away from Prague a decade earlier because of the horrible Leakage and now inhabited a Corp-owned estate in a quiet and influential section of Southern Munich. Our home was near the Bavarian Alps, owned by the Rhine Chemical Corp. My father was the group vice president. We were just over three-hundred kilometers from my beloved Prague, but well outside the contamination barrier.

"I was twenty-seven years old at the time and living in Paris, determined to make myself known in the literary world with my lean and biting poetry, but I had come home early in the holiday season more from starvation than parental respect. Marie arrived a week later and that's when I first saw Von Roon.

"He still had his right hand, then. It wasn't until he almost died in a skirmish during the Belt War that he assumed the use of a prosthetic controller. There in our happy home in Munich, he was charming, witty, and athletic. His back ramrod straight, his manner cool and confident. His hair was not so blond then, a fact which few people remember now, but his clear blue eyes could flash at you like sunlight on a silver shield. And his voice was so rich and assuring that I was certain he must have once been professionally trained as a holo announcer. My sister, of course, was deeply in love with the man, and I sometimes thought that my parents were as well.

"I suppose I should have seen him as a rival, some sort of challenge to my position in the family, but to be quite frank I didn't pay him much attention at all, at the time. I was too confident of my own grand destiny, too full of my own glorious future as a highly-respected writer to bother inspecting my sister's paramour. We had a nodding acquaintanceship, and I noted little of the man that I haven't already told you, except a brittle brilliance in his eyes and a sort of knowing kinsmanship about our shared ambitions."

જાજ

Chico came back into the room, carrying a collection of documents and a calculator. While they were organizing this material, a doctor whom Pat had never seen before stopped by to check on her condition and modify her treatment to relieve the nausea.

"You're improving ahead of schedule," he told her.

"So I guess the hospital won't mind all this clutter." He gestured to indicate the reports Chico had spread throughout the small room.

"Thank you, Doctor," Pat said. "I wonder if it would be all right if Ms. Kim stayed a little after visiting hours. We have a lot to do."

"I don't think that'd be a good idea," the man answered, "but you're free to leave your materials here as long as they're kept out of the way."

Chico sighed, as the doctor left. "Well, thank god I don't have to lug all this back to the office."

Pat picked up a handful of Vax printpads. "We haven't much time, so we'd better get started."

For the next hour, she read reports and signed forms, while her assistant balanced the books and issued payment for a multitude of expenses. When they had finalized the month-end accounting report for the two businesses, Pat asked, "Have you met this guy that Wolf was talking about?"

"He came in while I was at lunch. They were in the conference room for most of the day, but I was busy keeping tabs on our other operations."

"As an amateur psychiatrist, you'd find this case very interesting." The pain in Pat's head throbbed. She would have to stop and rest soon. "Send a Link to Wolf, so I can ask the patient a few questions."

Chico nodded and then froze as her mind meshed with the virus that permitted her to contact other carriers and establish communications. The tension drained out of the Korean woman, and Pat was about to pose a question, when Chico said, "Wolf says that Max is unconscious. He'll wake him up if you want, but I get the impression it was a real chore getting the guy to relax."

"What did he hit him with, a tram?" Pat sighed. "Oh, never mind. There's still a lot of info in the Vax report. See if Wolf can set something up for early in the morning."

Chico stiffened again, and Pat waited as her message was relayed to Archerson. When the Link broke, Chico stretched the kinks out of her back. "He's not crazy about early morning conferences, but he'll let us know if the patient wakes up. Are you sure that you don't—"

"No, I suppose we should get more of this office work done. Suppose we go on with it while the Vax plays. That way you can get a chance to see Mr. Maxwell Jannings for yourself."

Chico continued sorting several documents at the foot of Pat's bed. "Good idea,"

❧❧❧

"My first involvement with Von Roon came as the result of three significant events—my sister's marriage, my father's promotion, and my failure as a prose poet.

"Marie had married the man the following June. The wedding had been one of the most impressive affairs of the season, if you care about such things. I had never seen her happier, as were we all, I expect. Congratulatory messages came in from all around the world, and major corp execs arrived at the estate bearing gifts of great splendor and workmanship. I think that was the last time our family was truly happy together, and it certainly was the first time noted how high my father had risen in the ranks of the corps.

"It was also the first time I had ever spoken to Von Roon about anything other than trivial matters. We were alone together the entire evening before the marriage ceremony. There was no bachelor party. The man seemed to not have any close friends or relatives. I had been asked to be his best man and it seemed that part of this duty involved keeping the groom occupied until the wedding ceremony.

"We were lodged in what was then my family's summer cottage, a semi-rustic thing of glass and plasteel built into the side of Zugspitze Mountain, Germany's highest point. The cottage projected out from the mountainside into the crisp air fragrant with pines. I had an easy task before me, since Von Roon planned to use the time to rehearse a presentation he was to give the next morning to his social club, prior to leaving on a three-month honeymoon to New New York.

"Looking back, years later, I could see that this lecture meant as much to him as his marriage to my sister. It was an early version of his now-famous Creative Manifesto, wherein he identified the principles of Hope, Courage, and Productivity as the foundation for Earth's future. I had prepared to spend the night in the cottage entertaining the man with my poetry, but I was soon caught in the gradual unfolding of his words and ideas.

"Remember, this was almost two decades before the Belt War. Yet, even then, there was a stirring power in the content of his words and the ringing of his voice. I sat amazed by the man's poetic skills, something I immediately admired and envied.

"I had little or no interest in my sister's affairs, choosing to live my own life apart from my family on anything except the most important occasions. But that night, I could begin to see what she idolized in this man.

"His smooth, almost casual style of speaking pulled you along from assumption to proposition to conclusion with a skill of syntax that left me breathless. I was sure he must have given this speech many times before, but I later verified that this was a completely extemporaneous performance! He was merely speaking freely of his visions and dreams, weaving together words and phrases before a struggling poet who was taken up and carried along--as so many were later destined to be carried--by the sheer energy of his convictions.

"My feeble attempts later in the evening to counter his statements were deftly cast a side by him with a logic and elocution that spun my mind around and left me exhausted. By morning, I was nearly dizzy with new ideas and concepts. He, of course, seemed as fresh as if he'd just arisen from twelve hours of peaceful slumber. As soon as the wedding was over, I dashed from the reception and locked myself away in my room at the estate, intending to write the most wonderfully inspired prose I had ever dreamed of creating.

"But it was too late. Too much time had passed between my inspiration and the execution. The words just sat on the screen, unconnected by the magic of Von Roon's thoughts. I printed a copy and tried to edit by hand, hoping to revive their spirit and manually resuscitate their but without him, the words were only rude, jagged and dead."

∾∾∾

"You okay, Doc?" Chico set her reports aside and came up to the head of the hospital bed.

Pat kept her eyes closed and pinched the bridge of her nose. The pain was increasing. "Give me a minute."

"That man certainly rambles, doesn't he?"

"Yes, but his story is hauntingly fascinating." Pat sipped juice from a plex container and signed. "All right. Start it up again, please."

∾∾∾

"The second factor that led to my involvement with

the man was my father's sudden promotion that October, during the formation and reorganization of the new Weave Corp.

"The name Robert Jannings had been listed in the news several years earlier when Father was appointed Corpolitical Mayor of Munich as part of his GVP position with the Rhine Chemical Corp. The conjunction of business and politics was key to Earth's economic success during the twenty-first century. Without this conjunction, none of you Martians or other Outies could have ever colonized beyond the moon-bases or low-orbit stations."So, you can still see why we Earth people feel you owe much of your success to our financial sacrifices. The War settled all that for now, so I won't into it any further, except to say that while I now fear, detest, and loathe Von Roon and his Neo-Socialists, on this one point I cannot but agree: You couldn't be there, if we weren't here. We are—whether you like it or not—your heritage. I'll leave it at that."

⌘⌘⌘

Doc Pat shut off the Vax and turned to Chico. "I need perspective. Tell me what you think of all this?"

The other woman finished a computation and looked up. "You really want to know?" She didn't wait for an answer. "I think he's self-oriented and bordering on the psychotic, but you're the doctor."

"I thought so too, at first," Pat said. "It's his way of speaking. He's so informal, and yet I get the feeling this has all been rehearsed—"

Chico nodded.

"—but that could be an attribute of his frustrated desires to be poetic and maybe even part of his formal upbringing. He claims to be from one of the more-elevated classes of Earth people."

"He seems self-indulgent and a little dangerous, to me," Chico said. "And his shaking and trembling is creepy. Why don't we notify the gov and let them advise us of any outstanding warrants? I think we could use all the advice we can get on this person."

Pat pressed the side of her right index finger thoughtfully against her olive-skinned lips. "Call Arthur. See what he can tell us, but don't let him know that Jannings is holing up in Wolf's apartment. Use one of the outside com-units. I want to watch the rest of this on the Vax. "

"I'm getting hungry. Do you want me to order something to eat, while I'm out?"

"Hmm?" Pat looked up from her thoughts. "Oh, they should be along with supper soon. Tell a nurse that you'll be dining here with me tonight."

Chico set her papers to one side and rose to leave.

"Oh, and, Chico—"

She stopped at the door, looking back.

"Thanks, girl," Pat said. "You're good people."

Chico smiled. "I'll remember that when I want a raise."

"So, ask."

"Okay." Chico took a breath. "Can I have a raise, Doc?"

"As soon as I'm back on my feet—"

"Great!"

"—we'll talk about it."

"What a kind and thoughtful person—"

"I'm kidding. Of course you can have a raise. You deserve it."

Chico slumped where she stood in a display of relief. "I'll see about dinner and be right back."

Pat gave her a few seconds and then gingerly rose and walked to the bathroom. She was back in bed studying the Vax recording when Chico returned.

❧❧

"My father quickly rose on a wave of Neo-European patriotism, or rather Anti-Oriental suspicion, to a high-level of management. Through a series of buy-outs and mergers with French, American and Brazilian Corps, he ascended to the general managership of the newly-formed Weave Corp. This title gave him and our whole family a distinction in global politics, something akin to royalty.

"Weave Corp had evolved from an economic necessity of the Romantic and Teutonic-based peoples to exact their on the Oriental Zaibatsu conglomerates. A number of major political groups had banded together in this cause for almost three decades—ever since the Chinese/Japanese/Burmese Alliance that broke the Soviet's backs and nearly destroyed the world's economy back in the early part of the twenty-first century.

"This 'Unholy Alliance,' as it was justifiably called, left the rest of the world subservient to the Oriental economy. Differences in nationality and politics were put aside throughout the West, in order to scramble back from crushing poverty. Corporate dynasties were set up to pool resources in attempts that ultimately succeeded in defeating and destroying the selfish Orientals.

"Coincidental to this struggle, outposts like Achilles and Middle Spot on Mars and the ten settlements gained significant independence, while our attention was on pulling the Alliance snake from our economic throat.

"With the establishment of the Weave and its competing Volksfarbar Corp, an era of new prosperity began for the West. Not surprisingly, the Jannings family became regarded as a benevolent monarchy and my father was not only the chief corp exec, but also an influential political leader throughout the globe. It was in the latter position that he failed, however. Or, rather the public conscious failed him. A monarchy is an almost indefensible position, especially when productivity trends turn down. Having crushed the Oriental economic menace, there was nowhere else to go but off-planet.

"The problem was that you people had tasted too much independence and refused to remain allied to Mother Earth. These events did not occur overnight, of course, but the signs were there—clear enough for those who could read them—to see that some new form of government was needed.

"Many years before the Belt War, Eric Von Roon had installed himself in the more popular Neo-Socialist Party. At the time, I knew little of this. I chose to take advantage of my family's elevated position to devote my days and attention to poetics. Several of my books had been published, but none of them had brought me the fame or fortune I'd expected. This then, was the third factor of my involvement with Von Roon.

"Perhaps it was the monarchy syndrome, after all. I, like my father, had lost touch with the public. I wrote only the refined prose I thought would impress my peers. Whatever the reason, I admit failure now, as I did then.

"After my third book, *Siamese Twilight*, failed to attract positive attention, I succumbed to the family forces and joined the Weave Corp in the modest position of corp travel coordinator.

"Life as an exec was both exhilarating and exhausting. The responsibilities were heavy and at first somewhat frightening. There never seemed to be enough time to do all the work, but I soon found an ally in Von Roon. He was in authority over the transportation and communications divisions. Many of my assignments brought me in direct contact with him. After the first year, I was no longer afraid and, by the third year, I began to yearn for more authority.

"When the war came in '92, the corp underwent a massive re-organization. My father stayed at the top, but Von Roon became his second in command, overseeing budgets, logistics, and supply throughout the corp. I was elevated to Von Roon's former position with communications, where I quickly began pouring out the rousing messages designed to inspire the employees to greater heights of productivity.

"You would think that I would have been envious of Von Roon for being my superior, but I knew I had handicapped myself with my years of writing, while he had applied himself fully to his chosen task. He had even helped me ascend the corp ladder in what I took to be an open and altruistic manner. Of course, that was before I discovered these damn shakes you see my body going through—the long-term side effects of the Genezine drug he had been supplying me.

"No, in those days, I actually saw my father as the weakest link in the corporate chain of command. The taste of power was fresh on my palate when I would look at Robert Jannings and cringe at the thought of wasted opportunity. I had no clear understanding of system politics. To me, it all seemed quite simple—if one had the power, one should use it!

"Von Roon and I would talk of the misspent effort

with regard to the Outie colonies. Yes, I freely admit that, at the time, I was very much against your independence. It seemed to me that, if my father's primary duty was to hold the people together, then he should use all the force at his command to do so.

"But Von Roon saw things differently. His idea was to centralize the basic power of the people in a political party which he would head. He explained much of his Neo-Socialistic beliefs to me in private, knowing I would never pass them on to corp officials for fear of losing my drug supply. This was the beginning of the Axis Politi-corp."

∾∾∾

Chico and Pat dined on hi-pro hospital fare and discussed Maxwell's testimony.

"It's definitely a case for the textchips," Pat said, munching on carrot-flavored peco-paste. She hated the taste, but ironically it was the only thing she could stomach. "I could write a doctoral thesis on this patient."

"You don't believe what he's saying?" Chico asked.

"I'm sure there's *something* to it all. It'll take months to separate the truth from all his paranoid delusions. Then the withdrawal symptoms—he's displaying a confusing jumble of beliefs. We'll probably never know what's true and what isn't."

Chico poured the last of the McCoffee into both of

their glasses. "Then why don't we forget it for now and get the rest of this accounting done?"

"You're right."

Chico stretched. "God, I'm getting tired."

"How's the baby?" Pat asked.

"The doctors say he's coming along fine."

"Have you told Wolf?"

"No. Not yet."

"He'll be all right," Pat said. "Just be honest with him."

Chico hesitated. "He has so much on his mind, lately."

Pat snorted. "Was that a joke about his mods or the Link?"

"You know what I mean. Those voices he keeps claiming to hear."

"They're just a manifestation of his guilt. You know how I can tell they're not real—I mean, not from any outside source? They lack detail. Random delusions like Wolf's are vague and unformed. He'll get over Jonny's death and the voices he thinks he hears will fade away."

Chico nodded, but her eyes were on her food.

"But that's not the case for Maxwell Jannings," she mused. "His wealth of detail is fascinating. The war, Von Roon, Weave Corp, and now Axis. All of them can be easily referenced for comparison with standard historical texts. So, why would he base his fantasies so solidly on reality?"

She turned the Vax back on.

ഹഌ

"I see suddenly that I have rambled on into a confession of sorts. The only thing I haven't told you about is my sister's suicide.

"You see, Von Roon is a wizard at finding your weakness and using it against you. His bi-sexuality didn't bother me. I could handle that, but it was his ruthless adaptation of any method, any means to achieve his goals that finally alienated me. I'm sure it affected Marie in the same way.

"Looking back, I can see that Von Roon must have originally intended to rise to power through my sister's position within our family. He never loved her, nor did he give her children. To him, she was only a means to a greater end, and when I joined the corp, he immediately saw his way was blocked by my right of succession.

"Why he didn't kill me then, I'll never know. Perhaps he enjoyed our little talks, for I was easily persuaded to his way of thinking. Now that I was committed totally to the corp, nothing seemed illegal in the cause of profit. Von Roan displayed his theories openly to me and admitted to practicing ambush, assassination, and industrial espionage to get what he wanted. He appealed to the workers, supplying them with a false sense of justice. He ignored my sister, and I think she took the overdose out of loneliness, if not some crude sense of revenge.

"Her death meant little to Von Roan. Within a week of her funeral, he began showing even more attention to me.

"I accepted his invitation to attend an Axis meeting and was soon involved in implementing that party's greatest achievements. In a small monastery in Northern Japan, specially assigned monks had tended three cryogenic chambers for more than 150 years. The bodies in these chambers had been faithfully preserved, monitored and nurtured throughout the decades, enhanced by each improvement in medical technology.

"Within the three chambers slept the descendants of major World War German military officers, their minds and spirits expanded by a combination of mystic rites and electronic com-links.

"Von Roan had learned of this special facility and its inhabitants from the man who'd controlled the Neo-Socialist party in the late '70s. He investigated its existence and later channeled additional funding to the monastery from Weave Corp's logistic operations. One evening after he was sure I was rooted in the Axis cause, we took a private low-orbital shuttle to Kyoto and then journeyed by surface car into the Hokkaido Mountains. There, during what was ostensibly a Weave Corp trade mission, I was amazed to find that he had installed himself as head of this Oriental sect.

"'It wasn't just the funding that bought their allegiance,' he told me. 'I myself forged a file that proved to them that I was a fifth-generation descendant of an old, important German leader, Hermann Goring. They respected this since the three sleepers are the secret sons and daughters of Officers Rommel, Goebbles and Himmler.'

"The names meant little to me at the time, but research will show you that these people were part of an elite group of political warriors known during the World War as the Master Race. In the mid-1940s, when Old Germany held a treaty with Japan, these three young Nazi specimens were sent to the monastery as a secret investment and experiment in the future. There they were trained in mental, physical and spiritual abilities under a new scientific system that combined cryogenics, bioconductivity, and sensory deprivation.

"I realize all this is more than you expected from my testimony, but you must believe me when I say that the three known as Crusher Cloud, Spirit Lock, and Shadow Stone represent Von Roon's penultimate threat to the freedom of all mankind. They are completely under his control. He has managed to affect their consciousness so that they will do whatever he commands. This was his revenge against the major party officials who scoffed at his plans, calling them the Ninja Nazi Zombies!

"There was little scoffing, however, the night after Von Roon first employed his agents against all who opposed him—including my father.

"Less than a year ago, Robert Jannings was killed while on a hunting trip in the Black Forest Reserve. His body appeared to have been gutted by a wild boar, but I soon learned the truth: Von Roon had his warrior agents stealthily assassinate my father, so that I would ascend to the general managership of Weave Corp.

"I held that position for only one month. A month of terror, because I knew that I was next in line for Von Roon's murderous attack. I tried to rally the Corp's forces to dismiss him, but he was an opportunistic charmer and had placed his roots deep in the company's organization. Only a few eager, young execs supported me, and most of them were quickly and mysteriously dispatched, never to be heard from again.

"I fled to a backwater village in India, where I've hid for nearly a year, trying to overcome the damned withdrawal symptoms of Von Roon's vicious Genezine! I've kept a surreptitious watch on him as he has consolidated the Weave Corp and Neo-Socialist Party into the most powerful Politicorp on Earth.

"I escaped the planet only a month ago, after hearing from a secret contact that Von Roon doesn't intend to limit his power to the boundaries of Mother Earth. I understand from news reports that your company was almost able to stop him from securing the experimental bio-substance cultured by Blue Star Industries. There is something about the conditions on Mars that necessitates his using the fluid substance here. He wouldn't prize it so highly unless it could provide him with enough power to rule every person in the system.

"I've come to you for help and to alert you that he will be forced to return to your planet in order to perfect the use of this substance. He will undoubtedly take this opportunity to destroy you and your associates. If you will protect me, I will assist you in stopping him before his power and influence threatens any more lives.

"You cannot defeat him without my help. Believe me, he is ruthless beyond imagining. His greed is without limit! He will stop at nothing to kill us all, or make us his slaves!"

∽∾∽

The message on the Vax ended.

"This is the most fascinating and frightening case of ego mania I've ever encountered," Pat said. "I don't know whether to certify him or have him deported."

"He's dangerous, Doc," Chico counseled. "How does he know so much about our operations?"

"There's so much traitorous about his story, I don't think we can trust him. Make a few notes, and I'll call Wolf in the morning." Pat's pain was starting to intensify. She took a neuro-sedative and slipped under the covers of her hospital bed.

"You're the boss."

"And pile all that stuff up in the corner. We can work on it again tomorrow."

Chico did as she was instructed.

"Thanks, girl. You're always there when I need you." Pat nestled down in the bed, obviously exhausted. "And you've earned your raise. Take care of that baby."

Pat drifted off to sleep as her assistant left the room.

ʚঔেঔ

Chico walked calmly out of the hospital and caught a tram back to the Tripleye offices. She unkeyed the lock and went inside, carrying several files of completed reports.

The office was empty. It was late in the third shift and all the other ops had gone home.

*There's a traitor all right,* she thought. *But it's not the person Doc suspects.* She rubbed the back of her neck to relieve some of the stress that had gathered there. *I can't believe he let Jannings escape Earth.*

Carefully and confidently, she typed out a brief report on the man's ravings. She pressed a series of keys on the Vax and her report on the ex-patriot was sent to Weave Corp in New Berlin.

*This is the last time I help Von Roon.*

# CHAPTER 5

*XENOGAMY*

The bubbling swelled in her consciousness, causing Chico Kim to slowly rise from a heavy, fitful slumber.

She killed the alarm and automatically erected her mental shields.

It was ten o'clock in the evening, and Chico remembered dreaming of dark blue oceans and dull green hills. Somewhere.

Three hours ago, feeling depressed and alone, she'd stretched out on Doc Pat's therapy couch, hoping to lose some of the weariness that had amassed in her body like excess water.

But even after resting in the subdued light of the agency's office, she still felt sullen and now a little guilty at the thought of the mass of reports that needed consolidation.

For three weeks, while Doc convalesced in the hospital, Chico had kept tabs on Link Central, doing her best to oversee the operations of Intensive Investigations, Inc. This double-shift workload was beginning to gnaw at her nerves.

Tripleye's other ops were polishing off a number of minor but detailed investigations. Wolf had tracked down a disgruntled design engineer at Achilles Chemical, identifying the man as the originator of a compuvirus that almost wrecked the company's accounts receivable department. St. Mathew had gone undercover for the Martian military again, this time to gather info on a seditious commander of the Belt Guard who planned a coup involving the off-planet armed forces.

All of the field ops seemed to have an aversion to data recording. Like action-oriented children, they left the careful filing of information—necessary for proper billing and future reference—for someone else to struggle through.

Lately, Chico had begun to doubt that St. Mathew could still write a complete sentence! After an hour of "creative interpretation," she finally had something that made sense—she hoped. Now she could turn her attention to the scheduling of Doc's other business, the counseling of psychiatric patients.

Ironically, she realized that she, herself, might benefit from a little psychiatric help. It wasn't just the dull workload that was overcrowding her life, it was the constant lies.

Her deception couldn't go on much longer. Last week, when she had Vaxed her report to Von Roon advising him of Janning's arrival, Chico had promised herself that it was the last time she would update him on the Link, or Martian Gov and Corps, or anything.

After all these years, there was nothing lift in her to give him. Besides, Tripleye had been damn good to her, had trusted her, and she hated—absolutely hated—seeing it affected by Von Roon's influence.

It was almost midnight, and she realized she had worried away her most productive hours. Her slim body felt off center from the effects of the pregnancy. She was nearing exhaustion, and the work wasn't even half finished!

A sudden message from the Link took hold of her, tightening her muscles and frosting her vision.

'*Chico!*' Wolf's voice called in her mind. '*Get over here quick! There's a tall, thin man trying to take over my—*'

The Link released her abruptly. She tried to call back. '*Wolf?*'

There was no answer.

She tied again with the same results. He was supposed to be at his apartment, keeping an eye on Jannings. *Is this some sort of test? Does he suspect what I've been doing? Or, is he really in danger?* The fact that he didn't respond to her linking suggested he was unconscious.

Trying to stay calm, Chico struggled to decide what to do. She told herself that Wolf was a pro, a tough guy. And that made her all the more uncomfortable.

❧❧❧

The third shift at the sand mines had let out, so Chico sat crowded in with dusty, gritty passengers on a tram moving in the direction of Wolf's apartment.

In addition to everything else she had to manage while Doc was on the mend, Chico was the agency's backup in emergencies. St. Mathew was of little help, since he operated independently and could only be found when it suited him. Wolf was the strongest, most-experienced member of the agency, but if he was the one who'd gotten into trouble, what was she expected to do?

Investigate?

The tram slowed at the interSection near Wolf's corridor and Chico hesitantly stepped down. This was not the best part of Achilles for a pregnant woman to be wandering about in after midnight, one of the older corridors with poor ventilation and irregular support beams.

The light from the pizos and was dimmed by layers of dust and scum. Trash had collected in the corners of the interSections. Chico recalled that Wolf spent most of his credits on wine and jazzblues mods. Where he lived didn't seem to matter, as long as it was warm and enclosed.

The door to the op's apartment was slightly open. She held back for a moment, trying to mentally Link to Wolf for the fifth time since locking and leaving the office.

*'Wolfy? Can you hear me? I'm right outside your apartment.'*

Nothing. She swallowed dryly and rubbed her palms against her thighs before taking a deep breath and entering.

The room was a shambles. But that was somewhat typical of its occupant. There was a litter of small items—data chips, cleaning supplies, food packets, and clothing scattered under foot and on top of most of the furniture. Then she saw the leg.

"Wolf! Oh, god, what happened?"

He was hunched in an awkward fetal position between the bed and the wall. She felt a strong pulse and patted him down for his data modules. They were in a pouch on his belt. She gnawed her lower lip to relieve her anxiety and scooped out a handful of the multi-colored mods, hoping to find one that contained a standard stimulus program.

Chico made her choice and inserted a dark blue mod, labeled "Base Brain," into the top-slot in the bald op's head. Wolf sat up almost immediately, saying, "Jesus, kid! Can you still hear me?"

Chico jumped back. "It's me, Wolf. What happened?"

Wolf rubbed his temples. "I was talking to—" He stopped, letting his eyes scan the room. "Where's Max?"

"You mean Jannings? I thought you were watching him. Did he do this to you?"

"Nah," Wolf said, coming to his feet. "It was a tall, thin guy. Dressed in dark clothes and he had those weird eyes, again."

Chico didn't know what to think of that. "You've met him before?"

"No, but I've met the other one, Crusher Cloud. They both have the same zombie eyes. I think he hypnotized me, or something."

"Wolf, are you sure you're all right? Maybe we should check in at the hos—"

"No time." Wolf jammed a fedora onto his bald head. "We've got to get to Blue Star Industries. Fast." He strode to the door without looking back.

Chico stood her ground. "Wolf!" He stopped and looked back at her. "What the hell is going on here?" she demanded.

He gave her a hang-dog expression. "A guy came to the door. Said he wanted to see Maxwell Jannings. I told him there was nobody here by that name, and he should go jump on his thumb. He smiled and started looking at me in a way that froze me, like the Link. I tried to call for you, and the next thing I know you're here and Maxwell's gone. Did you Link to St. Mathew?"

"I couldn't find him."

"Figures. Come on. We've got to go!" He went out the door.

Chico shook her head in worry, but followed him. "Where are we going?" she asked as they hurried down the corridor to the tram stop.

"I told you," he said gruffly. "Max said that Von Roon and his goons would have to go back to BSI in order to get the info they need for their takeover."

A tram screeched and slowed as they jumped on. The shift change was over, so they had the vehicle to themselves. "What's Max got to do with Von Roon or Weave Corp's takeover bid for BSI?"

"I don't think its BSI he wants to take over," Wolf said.

"Who?"

"Von Roon."

"Well, what then?"

Wolf shrugged. "Max said they're after the entire planet."

She stared at him with the blankest expression she could muster. "How can you believe that? Doc says that Max is certifiable."

"Then answer me one question," he said. "If it ain't true, why'd they take him?"

೧൧೮

The electric tram dropped them at the front entrance to Blue Star, where Wolf signed them through security.

BSI was known for its advancements in micro-grav rice and other food stuffs. He had been on assignment at the Corp ever since the bio-substance theft several weeks ago. Doc Pat's hospital stay was the direct result of a sabotage attempt at one of the company's geo-therm stations. Tripleye was doing so much business with BIS lately, that it was beginning to feel like they were a subsidiary.

Wolf led the way through a sequence of offices, arriving at the company's R and D lab.

Third shift was in full swing and the crowded work area was elbow-to-elbow with stoop-shouldered employees inspecting data streams and performing intricate operations in real time.

Chico still wondered what all this had to do with Max. Wolf was Tripleye's best op. In fact, he had originally owned the agency until Doc Pat bought him out, but right now he seemed to be marching to a beat only he could hear.

She wanted to tell him what she knew, but she couldn't—yet. Soon, though. Maybe tomorrow. Or the next day. Sometime when we're not so involved with other people's problems.

"Zeke, this is Chico Kim," Wolf said to a short, dark-bearded man who wore thick, round glasses on the fat bridge of his nose. "She's with me. Chico, this is Yezd Abotai. We need to talk to you about the Snot."

The lab tech's eyes narrowed behind the heavy lenses. He jerked his head to the right. "Come," he said. "My office."

They turned a corner and filed into a cramped room. "This piece of work," Yezd said, walking around to a chair behind a desk cluttered with more paper than Chico had ever seen in one place, "is not for me. But—" He smiled. "I listen."

"Cut the crap!" Wolf answered. " You know Tripleye's been on contract ever since Skye Williams got the Snot away from you two months ago. We need you to tell us what the hell it is, if you ever expect to—"

The researcher raised his hand. "I make no compromises."

Wolf hefted a heavy data chip from a storage file. "Look, Zeke, we've gotta know what we're looking for, before we can find it. Things are starting to get serious, and I want some answers!" He slammed the data chip down on the desk.

Chico watched the dark-haired man's expression. It didn't change.

"I know it's confidential," Wolf conceded. "And I know I promised to work on the case in the dark, no questions asked. But my best lead was shanghaied only an hour ago."

The dark-bearded man smiled. "You are the most colorful talker I have ever met."

Wolf looked ready to explode.

'*Let me try talking to him,*' Chico linked, "Mr…" She suddenly realized she'd forgotten his name.

"Abotai," he supplied, obviously more pleased to be conversing with an attractive woman than a stalky, bald, brow-beating man. "Call me Yezd." He glanced disapprovingly in Wolf's direction.

"Yezd." Chico shook hands with the short lab tech. "Sir, I'll be honest with you. If we don't get more info on your bio-substance—"

"Snot," Wolf growled.

Chico ignored him. "—then you'll probably never see it again. Surely Tripleye has earned the respect of your company. Only weeks ago, our owner almost lost her life aborting a terrorist attack at your geo-therm station."

Yezd stroked his short, coarse beard. "Very well. I will make a call." He keyed the Vax and contacted his supervisor, explaining the situation. Permission was granted to reveal the basic facts in order to broaden the investigation's possibilities.

'*Nice going, sweetheart,*' Wolf linked, slipping a mod into his fontanel to record the new data as Yezd explained it.

The research tech tapped a sequence into his compad. "I will be brief. The bio-substance is the only known discovery of life on Mars. We found it during a site-inspection of a new fissure that recently opened up on the Xanth Plains. There, we discovered more of those ancient ruins, and this." The computer's screen presented a complex chemical structure which looked to Chico like a delicate growth of living crystal. "Physically, the substance is a greenish-yellow fluid at room temperature—"

"Hence, its name," Wolf said.

"Yes, but officially it is known as an electro-polyplasma."

"What does it do?" Chico asked.

Yezd rubbed the back of his neck. "From all we could tell, before it was stolen, the bio-substance seemed to be a living, thinking organism. It appeared to store information on the molecular level, like DNA. The few dominant genes remain unaltered, but the recessive ones could conceivably stockpile all the data currently in existence."

"Sure, Zeke," Wolf said, "and then it could sit up and talk to you."

"My instincts tell me that this substance has the potential to rearrange its cells in order to accommodate new info. You could actually watch it think."

Chico chose her words carefully. "Mr. Abotai, you're talking about life. Several companies have investigated the remains of the original Achilles civilization here in the city and they've found nothing at all like your bio-plasma."

"My good woman, every second corp on Mars would like to find some sort of life on this planet, but they have been looking in the wrong place for the wrong thing. Before God, I tell you that I watched this substance flow into the tiny crevasses and cracks of a data chip and absorb all the info from the circuits."

"Look, pal," Wolf said, "you still haven't told us why anyone would want to steal it. What's it good for?"

The researcher's dark eyebrows shot up. "What's it good for? Don't you understand that it just might have the potential of communicating with us by way of a computer interlink? That means this…this…"

'*Don't say it,*' Chico linked to Wolf.

"…living computer, might teach us about the original Achillians, or the process of life, itself? We've searched the site for additional samples, but have found none. This might be our only chance to explore this remarkable substance."

A thought occurred to Chico. "How do you know it's indigenous to Mars? Couldn't it have come from somewhere else?"

"Exactly that," Yezd said. "We don't even know how it came to be in the Xanth site, but it's a good wager that the original Achillians were aware of it, perhaps even employed it, because the cavern was full of the ruins of their crude, rockwall living quarters."

"So, let me see if I've got this straight," Wolf said. "We've got a greenish-yellow ooze that the Old Folks left us—maybe. And it can talk to computers—maybe. And Skye Williams stole it by having contacts with your disposal services. Right?"

This last point was new to Chico. "She was a trashhauler?"

Wolf nodded, and so did Yezd. "Unfortunately," said the dark-haired man, as he removed his glasses and pinched the bridge of his thick nose, "the substance was spirited away in one of the black stasis canisters we use for confinement of toxic substances. And, that, by the way, is all Mr. Archerson has been able to find out for us."

"If you'd've told me half of this in the beginning," Wolf bristled, "I might have had a clear shot at finding your goddamn bio-snot. But now—"

Chico jumped in. "What Mr. Archerson means is, we now have a good lead to cross-reference with our other info, and the possibility of locating your missing substance is much greater than before. It always pays to tell everything. Even the smallest details sometimes make a great difference."

"Indeed, it is results I want." Yezd got up and walked them to the door of his office. "I am glad I was able to assist you in discovering a clue. I am eager to learn of your results."

As the two ops were leaving the BSI operation, they paused while Wolf linked, *'He wouldn't recognize a clue if it spit in his beard.'*

⌘⌘⌘

The plan to locate Max was now coupled with the new information that Weave Corp was somehow involved with a revolutionary biological discovery.

"The case is heating up," Wolf said. "We'll need all our forces on this one. I'll try and find St. Mathew, while you update the gov. Call Art McBain when you get back to the office."

They had been walking down a corridor together, when Chico stopped suddenly. "I can call Arthur from any public Vax. I want to go with you."

Wolf put an arm around her, comfortingly. "And I want to go with you too, sweetheart. But where I'm going is no place for a woman in your condition." He patted her stomach. "I've played around with my mods in the last few days, and I think I've figured out where Jules St. Mathew spends his nights."

A tram rolled by and Wolf helped her on board.

"Take care and link to me if you find anything new at the office," he said as the tram rolled away.

She wanted to go with him, but she was relieved not to have to shield herself from his every gaze. Lately, it was all Chico could do to mask her thoughts from the telepathic communication that went on among the ops. She constantly had to guard against their accidental uncovering of her secrets.

A few weeks ago, Doc had finally decided to join the

Link, taking Chico completely by surprise. Luckily, the bosswoman had been distracted by her discovery of Chico's pregnancy and the wonder of linking to two minds at once. It had confused her enough for Chico to shield her deceit, once again. Within another second, Doc would have learned everything about her assistant's affair with Von Roon, but the truth was still hidden.

Von Roon had been Chico Kim's first, great love—the man who had saved her at a terrible personal cost during the war back on Ceres. But then he had left her, telling her she would be safer with Dr. Mishko. For more than a decade after, Chico had never stopped yearning, feeling drawn to a life that might have been.

Now, she had to guard every thought from possible reception by the other ops on the Link. Even simple decisions and passing impressions had to be muted and reconsidered. Where to file data? When to schedule assignments? How to respond to questions? The strain and fear were tearing at her mind and heart.

The absolute worst moment had come when Maxwell Jannings appeared on Tripleye's doorstep. Chico recognized him at once as Von Roon's number two man at Weave Corp. Fortunately, Jannings had never met Chico, so there was no possibility of him identifying her. He had escaped to Mars from Von Roon's influence, and the turncoat would rave to anyone who would listen about the "insidious Neo-Socialists."

Chico had worked carefully—even to the point of altering reports on Weave Corp's local operations—to persuade her boss to ignore the man's wild charges. Doc had discounted most of what Jannings said as a paranoid delusion, diagnosing him as mentally unbalanced. But because she was so fascinated with Jannings's behavior, Doc had asked Wolf to keep the man sequestered for further observation as soon as she fully recovered and could return from her stay at the hospital.

Chico knew now that her report to Von Roon must have been the cause of Jannings's abduction from Wolf's supervision. She didn't want him to see the guilt in her eyes.

The tram decelerated gradually and dropped her at the office at five thirty-seven in the morning. She felt dead tired, dreading the work that still needed completion before Doc's arrival.

Chico sighed heavily and unlocked the office door. *Why do I put myself through this? Is it some sort of self-punishment for betraying the agency's trust?*

There, piled in a sloping stack beside her desk, were the accounting chips from last month's audit. Scattered across her desk were patient files, message slips and the blank appointment schedule for Doc's psychiatric practice that she'd been working on when Wolf's Link had hit her. The Vax displayed her report on St. Mathew's investigation on Vegas station—

Chico felt a sudden chill. '*How did that get out?*' She glanced quickly at the alarm system. A tiny amber light told her that the office's security had been broken. Her pulse raced. *'Oh, god. Someone's been in here.'*

A movement in the shadows at the corner of her eye. She started to scream, adrenaline jolting her heart. But the eyes of the person in the darkness took hold of her, made her rigid, like the Link.

"Calm," a soft voice said. "Be calm. You are in no danger."

Chico wanted to run. Her muscles ached with tension, and then a warm wave of relaxation moved over her. She dropped to the floor as if she'd been clubbed.

Her perception of the approaching figure was skewed by the tilted angle of her head. She strained to sit up, but her body refused to respond.

"You are at peace, now," the figure said, bending over her. It was a tall, thin man, dressed in a black, loose-fitting body suit. His eyes were dead and cold, but they held her attention like twin electromagnets. His voice was velvet. "I'm going to help you up, now. We have very little time and much to discuss."

Chico felt herself settle in a chair. The thin man hovered over her awareness.

"My name is Henry Rommel. In Weave Corp, I'm known as Spirit Lock. You know Weave Corp and Von Roon? Yes, then you have nothing to fear."

*I can't move. I can't get away. I can't—*

"I sense you wish to speak. Be calm and keep your voice quiet."

Chico throat felt as if it was being released from a death grip. "You're one of the elite agents Jannings warned us about. I'm not your enemy. I'm the one who alerted Von Roon that Jannings was here. What do you want from me?"

The man smiled coldly. "And yet, I sense a deep trouble in you. Something stirring, something dangerous. My power goes beyond the simple ability to hypnotize. I can feel your hesitance, your doubt."

"No. You're wrong."

"But it is exactly as Von Roon suspected. Your association with the people of this world has weakened your resolve." He turned away to inspect the data on the Vax.

Chico made a faint attempt to Link, and the eerie man rotated back to deaden her will.

"Ah, yes. There, you see? I knew you couldn't be trusted."

"I didn't do anything."

He shook his head. "The Link. The famous Link that I've heard so much about." He came nearer her face, as if trying to see inside her skull. "You know, of course, that you really don't need it. Everything is perfectly all right. Besides, we have your friend St. Mathew—Shadow was insistent on his abduction—and we shall soon have Archerson and the rest. Von Roon is most unhappy."

She gazed deeply into those dead eyes. "You've no right to do this to me," she whispered. "I've been loyal to the man for almost thirteen years."

"He understands your loyalty and appreciates it, but we cannot risk further exposure to your friends in the gov. This agency has been too involved in our operations of late, and the suspicion is that you are part of this interference."

Her mouth felt dry as dust. "I've done nothing to hinder your operations. I've kept my place and reported on events efficiently as they occurred. I've created no interference of any kind."

Spirit Lock chuckled. It sounded like loose dirt tumbling into a grave. "Interference is why I'm here. This virus that lets you Link to others, I want a sample."

Chico felt herself being released. She rose dully and unlocked a drawer containing squibs filled with the virus. She gave a handful of the gray tubules to the tall, dark man.

"Very nice," he said, putting them into a fold in his loose clothing. "But I still sense resistance in you. Von Roon doesn't want you dead, but a little alteration of your mind is necessary."

Terror swept through her.

"Look at me." His empty eyes filled her. "You will not be able to use the Link again. In fact, you will send out the same numbing consciousness I am now giving you. An emptiness of rage. You will interfere with all transmissions of this telepathic power. You will jam it with an emotional haze of hatred. Now, DO IT!"

Chico tried to use the Link, and discovered—

nothing. It was as if it had never been. She pushed her thoughts out to Wolf, St. Mathew, even Doc Emory, but there was no response.

"Ahh," Spirit Lock said with great satisfaction. "You see? There is only the emptiness now. Which is as it should be, correct?"

The Korean woman slowly nodded, her eyes beginning to brim with moisture.

"Now, in only a moment, you are going to sleep," he told her in a soft and assuring voice. "A deep, restful sleep from which you will not awaken for many hours. When you do, you will collect your files and arrange passage to Earth. Von Roon wants to see you there in his Berlin offices."

She struggled again to block his influence, but failed.

"From this point on, you will continue jamming this telepathic Link. You won't recall that I've been here, or anything about our conversation, but you will obey. Yes?"

"Yes..."

"Sleep."

A warm vision came back to her. A vision of the vast, blue water; rich, yellow beaches; and soft, green hills of home. Then the emptiness absorbed her smoothly. Bitterly.

☙❧

A voice bubbled into her consciousness, causing her

to slowly rise from a fitful slumber. She felt as if she'd been bludgeoned. Her body was thick, her brain lethargic.

"I said," the voice repeated, "are you all right?"

Her vision was blurred with drowsiness, but she slowly recognized the wide, dark face hovering over her. It was her boss, Doctor Patricia Emory.

"Uh…" Chico said through a dry, bitter-tasting mouth. Why was she so tired?

"Here, drink this," the black woman said.

Chico felt her hands wrap around a cup of spiced tea. She took a sip and tried to twist the kinks out of her neck.

"My god, girl!" The big-boned woman held her at arm's length. "You look terrible! Have you been working all night?"

Chico nodded, rose, and shuffled into the bathroom. "Welcome home," she mumbled, closing the door behind her.

She sat there a few moments, trying to collect her thoughts. Pregnancy was a bitch. Then she came alert when she remembered about Max's abduction. She had to tell Doc! But there was something else…

The face in the mirror mocked her. Its dark, slanted eyes seemed to hide a sinister secret. What was it?

She splashed heavy water on her face and peeled it off, taking the last of her sleepiness with it. When she came back into the office, she saw Wolf and Doc exchanging comments.

"…and I couldn't find St. Mathew, either," the hairless op said.

"I caught the morning news," Doc replied. "Von Roon has returned to Achilles for more business meetings with Amos Brew."

"Did he have that Crusher guy with him?" Wolf asked eagerly.

"I don't know. But check at the Brew Distributing Company. That might be where they've taken Max. "

Chico heard herself say, "And St. Mathew."

Wolf stared at her for a moment, then he turned back toward Doc. "I'll get on it right away." He came over and Chico a light hug. "This little lady has been working her butt off for you, Doc."

"I know," the black woman said. "I just gave her a raise."

"Congratulations, little mother," Wolf smiled.

"Don't congratulate me yet."

Doc Pat looked up from the stack of message slips she'd begun to sort. "Why not?"

"Because—" Chico felt hot tears swelling in her eyes. "I—I don't know." Her body shook with grief.

"Hey, now." Wolf lowered her into a chair.

Chico trembled, feeling as if someone were pushing on her brain. In her strange sorrow, she heard the old op say, "Something's wrong, Doc. I just tried to Link to her and all I got was…nothing."

Fear rose up in Chico's heart. That was it! She tried

to Link to Wolf, to tell him her feelings, but nothing happened. It was as if he weren't even there.

Pat knelt to look in Chico's eyes. "What is it?"

Chico shook her head.

Doc hurried to the drawer where the squibs were
stored. She took one and began administering it to the
back of her own neck.

"Are you sure it's okay to do that?" Wolf asked.
"Your doctors might not like you using the virus so soon
after your rad-scrubbing therapy."

The black woman nodded with certainty. "I've got to
see for myself why the Link's not working. There's a
possibility of xenogamy conflicts."

Chico caught her breath and rose from her chair.
"I'm sorry. I don't know what's the matter with me."

She heard Wolf ask, "What's a xenogamy?"

"Cross-fertilization."

"Huh?"

"Her pregnancy might be affecting the Link."

"Oh. Yeah."

Doc Pat looked frozen in concentration for a moment, and then she turned back Wolf in amazement.
"Nothing. I couldn't even get you!"

Wolf began to exchange mods in the slot of his shiny
pate.

Chico wanted to tell them everything. How she had
betrayed them to Von Roon. How she had lied about the
baby. But a force inside of her still held back the truth.

"I found something!" Wolf said. He held the first two fingers of his right hand to his temple, as he scanned the data on a module. "My old man's mods suggest a possible connection between Skye Williams and Brew Distribution. The data's over a decade old, but still worth following up."

Chico wondered why she felt so tense. It was as if all of her attention was fixated on some vast and vague emotional effort. She tried to free herself, but the haze continued to drift in her head.

"Sounds like it's worth looking into," Doc said. "But until we learn what's wrong with the Link, you'll need to have a backup. I really shouldn't be running around until I get my strength back, but—"

"I'll go with him," Chico said, almost automatically. Having committed herself to a definite action, she felt the haze clear a bit. *It's the indecision,* she thought. *Doubt and confusion and guilt are surrounding me.*

"Are you sure you're up to it?" Doc asked.

Her resolve strengthened, and Chico rose to her full height, affecting a guise of confidence. "Just a little morning sickness. I'm fine now. Let's go."

Wolf looked at her with concern. "Well—I don't know."

"I'm fine, I'm fine. Leave me alone!"

Wolf looked questioningly at Doc. "All right. If you say so." He shrugged.

Chico joined him in the doorway, just as the older

woman said, "I think it might be a good idea to have a little chat when you get back, Chico. I want to help."

"Whatever you say. Doc," she answered, following Wolf into the corridor. The time was nearing for her to make a final, critical decision.

⁓⁓⁓

They had rented a groundcar, to insure immediate and complete mobility. Wolf used his mods to locate and arrange for the use of an office in a semi-abandoned transport station across the tunnel from Brew Distribution. Chico wandered through the series of old and crumbling offices and storage rooms, getting the lay of the land, while Wolf went across the way to try and gain entrance to the Brew facility.

She peered around a support pillar as Wolf returned. It was almost noon.

"No luck," he said. "The place looks empty except for a few security guards who wouldn't talk to me. But I left a bug on one of them, so we can listen in and track them, if they go anywhere."

"What sort of bug?" Chico asked, feeling the excitement of the hunt building within her.

Wolf showed her a row of black, hair-like threads that he kept in his belt-pouch. "I put one of these on the back of the guard's head. Sticks like glue. It's another reason why I hate hair. You can never trust what you find in it."

The two ops listened to the voices picked up on the bug's receiver. Someone was being rudely questioned. "We know you're part of Tripleye," a voice said. "What the hell are you people after?"

Chico looked at Wolf, who unconsciously chewed his lower lip. Then she recognized St. Mathew's mocking tones coming from the receiver. "We believe in liberty and justice for all," he said. "But I can see that none of you know the meaning of the phrase, much less its origin."

"So this is where he's been all the time," Wolf said with little surprise in is voice. "Won't that guy ever stop grandstanding?"

"You folks know you haven't got a chance," St. Mathew continued. "Right now, a dozen of my associates are on their way here to rescue me."

"He's bluffing," Wolf said.

"You're bluffing," a woman's voice said over the receiver. "But we're not stupid. Charlie, bring the ground-car around front. Mr. St. Mathew is going for a little ride."

"That sounds like Williams," Wolf said. "This may be the lead we've been hoping for. I'll follow them in the rental and you get back to the office to let Doc know what's happening."

"Again?" Chico responded. "Doc sent me out here to back you up, not to run errands."

"Yeah, but I'm not so sure Doc knows what she's doing these days. She's changed. Haven't you noticed? She refused to believe me when I told her about hearing Jonny in my head. Said it was just guilt for my being involved with his death."

"You were not! If anyone knows why Jonny died, I do."

"How do you know? You weren't even there."

"According to Doc, Jonny was eager to prove himself. He had a messiah complex. He wanted to be a hero, regardless of the cost. If trouble came at him, he faced it squarely, daring it to back down. That's what made him so attractive, and that's what got him killed, not some dumb mistake on your part."

Wolf looked stunned. He was beginning to put it all together. "What do you mean, 'attractive'?"

A battered groundcar drew up in front of Brew Distribution. The driver got out and went into the building across the way.

"Ah, hell, Wolfy, I can't lie to you anymore. You mean too much to me." Chico stroked her swollen stomach and looked down. "This isn't your baby. It's—"

"Jonny's," Wolf said with certainty. A strange look came into his eyes. Chico thought he was on the Link, but that didn't seem possible. The bald op's expression drifted from sternness to resignation. "I understand now," he said. "Jonny just explained it all to me—about you two. He loved you very much."

Chico was rocked by this revealing statement. "Are you telling me you can still talk to him? My god, Wolf, that's…obscene!"

Wolf looked around anxiously. They were losing time. "I know it's hard to believe. I tried to explain it to Doc, but she wouldn't believe it either. Somehow Jonny's still with me." Clearly he wanted a way out of this conversation, but he also seemed to want to get it off his mind. "I don't know if it's because we were linked when he died and he's still in my head, or if the Link somehow channels me to him. But you see now what I've been dealing with, these last few weeks."

Two men and a woman came out of the entrance to Brew Distribution, guiding Jules St. Mathew toward the groundcar. St. Mathew wore a common laborer's jumpsuit and a gray wig. One of the security men shoved him into a storage compartment in the rear of the vehicle, and walked back into the building. The other man got into the front of the groundcar with the woman and started driving down the corridor.

Wolf took hold of Chico's shoulders and looked deeply into her eyes. "Listen, I don't care if the baby's mine or not. I mean I care, but somehow it's fitting that it belongs to Jonny. And that's all the more reason for you to keep out of danger."

"But you don't understand. I *need* to be helping on

this," Chico told him. "All I do day in and day out anymore is sit in that damn office and shuffle data. It's nothing like what you do, what Jonny did. You couldn't understand how important it is for me to do something that—that matters, something that makes up for—"

"We're wasting valuable time," Wolf said. "I've gotta get after that car. And you're going back to the office, whether you like it or not."

She wanted to tell him everything. She didn't want to tell him anything. She liked Wolf. She hated Wolf. She didn't know what she thought of Wolf. She hated herself for feeling like this!

"Please, Wolfy—"

He reached out and carried her into one of the abandoned offices. "I'm *not* going to let you get killed, too, kiddo."

She struggled as he set her gently on the floor and rushed back to the door, slamming it behind him.

Chico's eyes filled with rage. "You shithead!" The door wouldn't open. "Don't do this to me, Wolf!"

There was no response.

She spun around in a fury and discovered another door on the opposite side of the room. It led her into yet another, bigger room with several other open archways leading back to the storage center.

Seconds later, Chico came back into the room where she and Wolf had listened to the conversation. Searching further, she found that the rental car was now gone.

*Dammit! I'm not taking any more of this! They treat me like I'm nothing. I might as well not even be here.*

The thought rang clearly in her mind. She located a rear exit, walked three intersections over, still in a fury, and caught a tram to her apartment.

*I can't stand it anymore*, she thought, entering the small room and staring at her few possessions. *I'm through. I hate Wolf for his smug self-centeredness. I hate the agency for its stupidity. And, most of all, I hate myself for my own damn faithless treachery.*

Chico began stuffing essentials into a travel pack. Then she keyed her Vax to the Shuttle Services, intending to purchase a ticket to…

Where?

Back to the Belt, where she had grown up? Where she had met Von Roon? Where she and Dr. Mishko had first perfected the Link virus?

No, they would surely find her there. They were, after all, investigators. Besides, she wanted a clean break with her past.

If she were to truly start her life over again, she wanted a place completely different from anything she'd ever experienced. And, in order to escape detection, she would have to find a place so chaotic and teeming with humanity, that the agency would have little hope of ever detecting her.

Chico entered in her destination: Inchon, Korea, Earth. The instant she did it, she realized it was what she'd always wanted for a long time. She had decided to break with her recent past and re-invent herself.

Already she felt free. She sped to the shuttle terminal, thinking of green hills and blue oceans.

ೡೡ

The shuttle accelerated smoothly along its super-conducted track, and Chico held her stomach, feeling the G-force press against her. There were few passengers leaving for the Deimos Exchange Center, so she took a seat next to a trapezoidal window.

Now that she was away, she thought of calling Doc Pat and telling her what had happened to Wolf and St. Mathew. But Doc would want to know where they were, where she was. Couldn't the woman do anything on her own?

Chico felt relieved that the Link wasn't working. It was proof that the experimental virus still needed further investigation, but not in a situation where Doc could assume authority over it.

She suddenly found herself again hating the woman who had appropriated the Link project from Dr. Mishko and failed to see the truth about Chico's feelings, during all those long years. She was a psychiatrist, for sake, Chico fumed. She was supposed to understand what a person really thought.

*I hate them all,* she realized. *Doc and the others did*

*nothing but ridicule me, make me act like a coward. I could never tell them what actually happened in the Belt with Von Roon. To them, I was just Link Central, a message carrier, a way for Doc to know what was going on without risk in a silly business she had no right to be in.*

Well, Doc was on the Link now, for whatever good it would do her. She had finally faced her responsibilities to the other members of the agency. She'd taken the Link, overcoming her fears of harmful side effects. Maybe that had been the moment when Chico first began to doubt her own purpose, her own place in the organization.

*No! It's deeper than that.* It was back, years ago, when Von Roon had come into her life. When the Ceres station had been under command of the Dominion. They had controlled all operations in the Belt back before the War, until Von Roon had challenged the Dominion's rule. He had been held in confinement and his left hand severed away by her father as a demonstration of the Dominion's refusal to deal with the Inner-planet politi-corps.

Chico had freed the man and fled with him to the Triage Station. That was where her self-doubt began, she realized. He had abandoned her there, telling her she would be safe working with Dr. Mishko's experiments with the Link. Now, she hated Von Roon more than anything else.

She gazed out the window at the rolling limb of Mars. She began to relax and wondered casually why the

Link had failed. A standard application of the virus to a predisposed subject wore off in three days, but a sudden end to all mental transmission and reception by all parties—that was something new.

There was still so much they didn't know about the substance. The Martian Gov had sanctioned Tripleye to test the Link, to learn more about the potentially hazardous side-effects. But Chico had the nagging feeling that somehow she, not the Link, was the cause of this current break in communications.

A voice inside her spoke clearly to her consciousness. '*You are.*'

Her neuro-muscular system became rigid. '*Who's that?*' she thought. '*Is the Link working again?*'

'*No, Chico. Not the way it normally does. Please don't be alarmed. You might affect the baby.*'

'*Who is this?*'

'*Stay calm, dear. It's me. Jonny.*'

The excitement charged through her as she sat frozen in her seat. '*Jonny? Jonny's dead. How—*'

'*Well, there seems to be some question about that. My body is gone, but I can still talk to Wolf. It has something to do with the quality of the virus. It's neither dead, nor alive. It's…just something else.*'

'*But you're not linking to Wolf,*' Chico said. '*You're linking to me!*'

'*Almost. Actually, I'm linking to the baby.*'

The stiffness was beginning to collect in her joints.

She had trained herself to withstand the pressure, but the added shock of hearing Jonny's voice again tore at her endurance. *'I must be going insane,'* she thought despairingly.

*'No,'* Jonny answered. *'That's what Wolf thought at first, too. But I can reach around the mental blocks you've set up, because the baby is a part me and part of you. His DNA forms a bond between us that reunited the Link, even around your interference.'*

Chico didn't understand. *'My interference?'*

*'Yes, my love. You are the source. Don't you feel a portion of your mental energy filling the Link with your heavy emotions?'*

She attempted to understand her own mental forces. It was impossible, at first. But then Jonny went away from her and she relaxed. But not entirely. That was how she knew, suddenly, that he was telling her the truth.

"I'm the one," she whispered, feeling her stomach. "Something inside of me has taken away their ability to reach one another."

*'No,'* Jonny linked. *'You can still link to Wolf through me. Do you want to try it?'*

*'Yes,'* she said without hesitation. *'Do it. I have to talk to him.'*

*'Hey, partner,'* Jonny linked. *'How are you?'*

*'High and hard, kid,'* Wolf answered. *'So, you're back in my head again, eh?'*

*'I've got someone here who wants to talk to you.'*

*'Wolfy?'* Chico called to him.

*'Chico? Is that you?'*

*'Yeah, Wolfy. Where are you?'*

*'I'm in the rental up on the surface. I was following those turdbutts into the Xanth Plains, until you locked me up with the Link. How'd you get it working again?'*

*'Jonny says I'm the cause of the interference.'*

*'Hey, I hadn't realized. You're right. You can hear Jonny, now. It isn't just me. I told Doc I wasn't crazy!'*

The pain in Chico's muscles was increasing, but she didn't want to let go.

*'Someone's tampered with her mind,'* Jonny said. *'She's been sending out a steady flow of raw hate that's been blocking the Link's capacity to connect minds.'*

*'Well, tell her to stop,'* Wolf said. *'You hear me, girl? I'll bet it was the same guy who knocked me out with his eyes and took Max. These Weave people will do damn-near anything to get their way.'*

Outside her window, Chico saw the starscape turning as the shuttle aligned itself for docking. She realized that someone at Weave had tampered with her mind. Yes, she could still feel it. It must have been Von Roon. *'I—I don't know if I can stop the jamming.'*

*'Don't pull my dork, woman. You've got to! It's the only edge we've got against the opposition. Now, concentrate. I know you can do it!'*

*'He's right,'* Jonny said. *'Find your hatred and let it go. Nothing can hurt you now.'*

Again, Chico came off the Link. She sat with her eyes closed, searching for the source of her feelings. Von Roon had done this to her. She had to ignore the hatred, think about something positive, something that gave her hope.

She remembered telling someone that even the smallest details sometimes make all the difference in the world.

Small details. Little things. Like a baby. Jonny had said that it was a boy. She had Jonny and she had the baby. That gave her a new future and new hope.

Chico felt the tension draining. Her body relaxed and, for the first time, she felt the baby kick in her womb. "Oh." She laughed in wonder.

'*That's it!*' Wolf linked. '*I think I can get through to Doc. Doc, can you hear us? Doc, it's Wolf.*'

'*Yes,*' Doc Pat answered faintly. '*Where are you?*'

'*Out on the surface,*' Wolf said. '*We've located St. Mathew. A security guard from Brew and Skye Williams have him,. heading south west into—*'

'*That would put them—Xanth,*' Doc responded weakly. '*—to get Max—*'

'*I'm losing you,*' Chico linked. '*What's happening?*'

'*Chico. We can't—*'

'*Doc? I'm sorry, I can't hear you,*' Chico cried. '*Doc? I'm sorry!*'

'*Don't be alarmed,*' Jonny said. '*Your treatment is simply wearing off.*'

She realized it had been three days since she had taken the Link. '*But I can still hear you?*'

'*Yes. And I can get them connected back with you, if you wish. It's a little tricky, but—*'

'*No,*' Chico linked before she even knew why. '*It's enough to know that they are back together again. I've been weak, betraying them, exposing their activities to someone who wants to destroy them. They're better off without me.*'

'*You should go back and be with your friends.*'

Chico watched the shuttle pulling into port on Deimos. *No*, she thought, coolly controlling her rage. *I wanted to make a decision, and now I have. Someone has violated my mind, and now I know who. I'm going to make sure that Eric Von Roon pays for his years of toying with my life. I'm going to Earth.*

# CHAPTER 6

*XANTHIC EXIT*

Wolf remembered driving the ground car across the orange Martian plain, reflecting that he hadn't found out shit.

He'd tracked the Weave Corp security team that had hi-jacked his partner, Jules St. Mathew. And Chico somehow had gotten the Link working again, so he could send his thoughts back to Doc Pat. But all that seemed like dumb damn luck to Wolf, rather than the results of his skilled investigative methods.

Hell, at this exact moment, he wasn't even sure who he was following, or where they were going!

On top of everything else, it made filing a report on the new ultra-Vax a real bitch, especially now that things had fallen apart all over the city.

He slipped into report mode and began…

❦❦❦

A couple of small dust devils were kicking up dirt off to my left in an area known as the Xanth Plains. I kept my eyes on the surface car in front of me, watching it leave tracks in and out among the endless rows of eroded hills. There was a layer of haze hovering over the horizon. The sky was pink with diffuse sunlight.

I froze as Doc linked to me, almost piling up on a series of porous, russet boulders.

'*Wolf?*'

'*Not now,*' I linked back. '*I'm driving.*'

'*Hold up a minute,*' the boss lady said, and she broke the Link long enough for me to follow her command. I didn't want to lose my quarry and told her so.

'*It's important,*' Doc said in my mind. '*I've lost Chico. The Weave Corp people might have her, along with St. Mathew and Jannings.*'

That's when Jonny spoke up. It was getting a little crowded in my head. '*No,*' he said. '*Chico is gone. She won't be coming back.*'

'*What do you mean,*' I asked the kid. '*Gone? Gone where?*'

'*I can't tell you, partner. She made me promise not to. But, you shouldn't worry. She and the baby are safe and healthy.*'

Shit.

'*Hey,*' Doc linked. '*What the hell happened? I lost you for a second.*'

I decided not to hassle it out with the Doc. There would be time enough later to discuss with her my little voice that wasn't there. Right now I wanted to get back on the road, before I lost track of the Weave Corp security car. '*Listen, Doc,*' I linked. '*Chico's all right. She—she linked to me just before her treatment wore off. Don't worry about it now. I've got to get back on the trail of these guys. We're still heading southeast. Should be coming up to Selby station in another couple of klicks. I'll get back to you then.*'

Fortunately, she didn't answer, and my muscles and nerves unlocked enough for me to hit the accelerator and steer my way back across the billion-year-old plains. The dust devils danced among the distant buttes. I envied their freedom.

The tracks lead up to one of those freehold domes operated by quick-claim icespecters. I didn't know it at the time, but this one had been funded by Brew Distribution, a Weave Corp subsidiary. It looked like those guys were a lot more involved in the day-to-day activities of Achilles City than anyone would've ever suspected.

I didn't see their vehicle, but they'd been here, that was for sure. The tracks and other signs were all around the outside of the low, grey building. I twist-locked the gloves and helmet of my pressuresuit and popped the seal on the rented ground car, deciding to have a quick look around.

Once inside the station, I didn't have any trouble at all finding the body. He was a dark-haired, bearded man who had taken a mazer burn in the side of the face. He'd tried to get a message out on the Vax, but the screen only sat there waiting for a keystroke that would never come.

Twisting my helmet loose, I looked around the cluttered room. There were only a few signs of a struggle. Whoever fried him did it without warning. I wondered what the beef had been. Blackmail? Withholding info? Or, just tidying up loose ends?

As I started to drape a soiled rag over the poor guy's hairy face, I noticed the access port in the top of his head, just like me.

There was a blue plastic module still in his brain.

Apparently, the people who'd killed him—and I knew they had to be the same manufactured mothers I was tracking—had stolen the rest of his collection of mods, but they'd missed the one that was in his fontanel. I carefully worked it back and forth until it came free in my hand. It looked to be still in one piece and compatible with my own.

Right then, I knew I was going to try it.

A generation ago on Mars, mod technology had been a way of life. Today, what with the Vax system networking throughout all of Achilles, very few people took the trouble to have the operation that would allow them to slip in a data mod and access volumes of pre-recorded info. I had to admit that I didn't use it much anymore either, except to listen to jazzblues, or reminisce about the cases my old man solved before he died.

But this guy must have used it as insurance, a sort of back-up system to record the events that were happening around him. Someone had wanted to access his data, I figured, without his consent. They just didn't know he was recording when they burned him. Messy people.

Dropping the mod into the slot of my head, I sat down and started scanning. I would want to shut it off before I got to the end.

It didn't feel wrong. I'd expected a tweak or twinge of pain, but everything dropped right into place, just like one of my normal mods would. I knew that what I was doing was dangerous, but at the moment I could think of no better tactic. Still, I kept my hand on the mod, ready to extract it at any second. No fool, I.

It seemed that they were after info about the newly-opened fissure over at Achilles Fons. The dead mod user had been exploring there. He'd been on assignment from Eric Von Roon, himself. Apparently, the head of Weave Corp and the Neo-Socialists was extremely interested in the recent uncovering of a yellowish-green bio-substance that I'd been calling the Snot.

My mod user had played it cagey, as I'd suspected. He wanted more credit for his info, because he thought the Snot was more than just the remains of the Old Martians. He thought it was something that had come from outside the System, decades or centuries ago; something that had taken control of the Old Folk; something that had used them.

Skye Williams was the one who had killed the mod user. At least, she was the one who'd pointed a mazer at him when he'd refused to tell her exactly where he'd found the stuff. She said that Von Roon and his goons where flying down to meet them at the excavation site. She wanted the mod user to drive her over in his half-track. Then he could spill everything to Von Roon personally.

But he refused to cooperate. Skye pressed the mazer to the side of his face, and I exited the mod so fast, my stomach turned a little nauseous. It's one thing to talk to a dead man, like Jonny. It's another to experience it firsthand via a mental data module. It probably just went abruptly blank, but I wasn't interested right then in finding out.

I sat there in the middle of nowhere, trying to think it through. Skye was a smart woman. She'd been around the rough side of Achilles City for almost sixty years, and she knew all about how the data mods worked. I figured she had taken what mods she could find, after burning the hairy guy and then headed off in the ground car to the excavation site in the fissure.

No doubt about it, this case was screwier by the minute. First, a tall, black-garbed guy had hypnotized me and abducted Max Jannings from my apartment. Then St. Mathew had been stuffed into the back of a ground car and driven up here by Skye Williams. Now, Chico was missing and I had a dead icespector on my hands.

I decided this would be a great time to Link back to Doc and give her an update.

'*Keep after them,*' she advised. '*If St. Mathew hadn't let his basic treatment run down, you could Link to him for an update from his position.*'

'*Tell me about it,*' I answered. '*We need to have a talk with that young showoff.*'

'*I hear you. Wolf. And I'll handle it as soon as you two get back. Trust me.*'

'*Like a mother,*' I told her and broke the Link.

Back out on the Xanth Plains, I followed the track, driving the ground car as close as possible to the area where the new fissure had torn up the ground. The canyon lay fluted before me under a salmon sky. It was a nice image, I thought. A heavy wind was kicking up yellow dust from the surface.

I abandoned my rental car behind an ochre butte and worked my way forward on foot from dune to boulder. The fissure laid a ragged, kilometer-wide gash in the gritty lava plain. Several smaller cracks wound their way off in different directions.

Loose gravel and sand had poured down into the raw canyon, almost covering the jumbled collection of cliff dwellings that had been housed on the cavern before the fissure widened into a rude and dangerous furrow. It looked like the ancient Achillians had lived in simple masonry apartments, like the ruins discovered back in the cavern where the city stored supplies. There were plenty of sculpted openings in the outer faces of these rude buildings and on up to their tops, where the Old Folk must have used ladders of some sort to climb from room to room. I counted sixteen stories stacked in a jumble like children's blocks on finger-shaped plateaus below the rim.

As I watched, a group of vehicles worked their way down a rugged path to the center of this ancient and bizarre relic. I clambered down a side canyon, almost cascading on my ass under a precipitous wall, until I could move from one terrace level to another and get in close to where my quarry were gathering.

The vehicle containing St. Mathew drove into the wide mouth of an empty apartment three stories below me. Minutes later two pressuresuited persons strode out. One was too tall to be St. Mathew and the other was too broad in the chest and shoulders. I figured these two had to be a couple of Von Roon's ninja guys.

I linked back to Doc again, telling her what I'd found and to advising her to get some gov or security people out here quick. Then, cautiously and yeah somewhat stupidly, I searched around trying to locate a passage that would get me close to wherever they'd taken my captured pram-donna partner.

Peering carefully out of an apartment's ragged window, I caught a good glimpse of Von Roon, himself. He was flanked by two guardians carrying tech equip and heading for the flat roof of a block the size of a tram station.

I continued to search for St. Mathew, finally locating him three levels down, huddled and trussed up with adhesive cable in a shadowy room next to one other person. A quick climb over a broken wall and a turn around a narrow corner led me to the entrance of the darkened chamber. I knew this wasn't a good idea, but something in me wanted to approach them, wary of any hidden traps.

St. Mathew saw me coming, and I'd swear he winked in recognition.

The situation looked relatively safe. I got around the other guy and up behind St. Mathew and sliced the cable with a utility knife.

I had no idea what frequency his suit was set to, so I handed him a squib of the Link and motioned for him to stab himself in the heart.

He gave me a look of disgust and cycled the tube through the pocket in the side of his suit, administering it orally.

The other guy just sat there, but I could see that he was conscious enough to shift around, so I could cut him free as well.

It was almost a hundred years or ten minutes, depending on your frame of reference, before I felt the first stiffness of the Link and heard St. Mathew's snide voice in my head saying, '*Well, well. Look who's here: the Martian Manhunter.*'

I was ready with a response to his quip. '*The gaudier the patter,*' I linked, '*the cheaper the crook.*'

'*Max and I are on 122 MHz. Tune us in, so we can all chat.*'

I didn't like transmitting, but it seemed the only way I'd be able to talk with Max. I came off the Link and dialed the frequency with my chin. "I've got a ground car hidden outside. Let's move."

"Wait!" Max Jannings piped up. "We've got to stop Von Roon!"

"Stop him what?" I asked.

St. Mathew flexed his arms and legs. "Max says that Von Roon wants to set up the proper physical conditions to replicate the Snot."

"So? Look, can we discuss this later?"

"He only cares about himself," Jannings broke in. "He'll stop at nothing to get what he wants!"

"So what does he want?" I asked.

Jannings rose and stretched, almost stumbling in his haste to walk or run. "He wants to communicate with the bio-substance. He believes that it is the next stage of evolution, and that he and his pure-trained agents deserve to be Mankind's vanguard."

"The rest of us," St. Mathew added, "are just dirty scum to Mister Von Roon. What he's doing is probably illegal and possibly dangerous." He came to his feet and yelled. "Max get back here."

I reached an arm out and kept the guy from going any farther without us. "What's he doing here?"

My partner took time to dust himself off. "Max got kidnapped because he was trying to alert the authorities. I dealt myself in out of curiosity."

"Don't try and kid me. You were abducted! I saw your ass hauled out of the Brew facility. They stuffed you into the back of a—"

The ground vibrated slightly beneath our feet.

Jannings' eyes grew large. "He's started already. We've got to stop him."

I shoved Max toward the passage I'd come in through. "Look, you little malf, I've had about enough of your rantings. I'm in charge of this rescue operation, and I say we get our butts out of here."

"But, someone's got to—"

We couldn't risk continuing to communicate like this for fear that someone else might overhear our transmission. "Not us! I've already sent for help from the city security, so get moving!" I pushed him again, and he stumbled against St. Mathew.

"Come on," St. Mathew said. "Wolf may be rude and obnoxious, but this time he's right. Let the authorities handle it."

I finally got them out of there without being seen or, I hoped, heard. Just as we were climbing over a crumbling wall, one of the bad guys came around a corner and spotted us. He turned, as if to signal someone behind him, and then came straight ahead.

I recognized him immediately. He was the broad guardian guy I'd met before, the one who had killed Jonny: Crusher Cloud. "You two try and get to the top of the canyon. Keep to the left and you'll find the ground car. I've got a date with a zombie."

Even through the plex of our helmets, I could see his dead eyes. He pulled a nunchaku from behind his back and started twirling it all around him. I got my utility knife out and stepped toward him.

I let him get as close as possible, without getting my head chopped off with those spinning duralloy tubes, and then I switched the knife blade around in my right hand and threw it with all my strength at his wide, flat chest. It pierced the shithead's suit, sinking in to the hilt. The fact that he even wore a pressuresuit meant he wasn't really dead, I reasoned. So, maybe there was something I could do about that.

He staggered for a moment, and I took off in a direction opposite from Max and St. Mathew. I wanted to get away from Crusher, but not too far.

'*How you guys doing?*' I linked to St. Mathew.

'*I'm fine,*' he answered, '*but I've lost track of Jannings.*'

'*Get him on the radio.*'

'*Tried it. He doesn't respond.*'

*'Shit!'*

*'You okay?'*

I went off the Link and scrambled up to the roof of a fourth-level apartment. Hefting a couple of palm-sized rocks, I linked back, *'I don't know yet. I hurt him, but he isn't down.'*

*'I've got an idea,'* he answered. *'I ran into another of these weave-zombies on Vegas. She didn't know about the Link, and somehow I could tap into her mind.'*

My shoulder muscles were beginning to cramp up, but there was no sign of Crusher. *'Get to the point!'*

*'Hold on,'* St. Mathew said. *'I'll see if I can learn something through her that will help you take out your big buddy.'*

*'Hurry.'*

Crusher Cloud was moving around below me. One hand was held tightly over the spot on his broad chest where my knife had punctured him and his suit. He swung his nunchaku down, smashing helmet-sized boulders to gravel, but his movements were stiff, as if the cold was getting to him.

I heaved one of my rocks down at him, thinking, *You burned Jonny. Now I'm going to freeze you!*

The plummeting stone caught him in the right arm and made him drop his weapon. While he grabbed and ducked and tried to get a look at me, I felt the tightening in my muscles that meant someone was starting the Link.

'*Not now!*' I sent with firm conviction. '*I need to get the hell out of here!*'

My vision shook as the ground vibrated again.

'*I think I've got something that'll help.*'

'*Save it. Find Max. I'll call you back later.*'

Crusher had his weapon back and was starting to climb to my level.

I threw another rock at him, but missed completely. Looking around, I spotted another passage. This one seemed too thin for Crusher to get through. I scrambled toward it, feeling a sudden shock in the back of my left leg.

He'd caught me with that damn nunchaku. I fell forward through the entrance to the passage and tried to get up and keep going. *Come on, Archerson,* I hissed. *You're a tough guy. Let's see you stand up.*

Jonny linked to me. '*Hey partner, you all right?*'

'*Get off the fucking Link!*' I screamed. '*I've got to get out—*'

He was gone and I could move again.

Crusher was pushing and driving himself through the narrow opening.

I clambered up and hobbled to the other end of the passageway. There was a sharp turn and a worn set of stairs ascending to the next level. I crawled up, my leg feeling numb. A cluster of caution lights flared in my helmet.

I turned a corner and found the kind of situation St.

Mathew would have loved. A blank wall. Dead end with no way out. Not even a stone to throw at my advancing opponent.

'*St. Mathew*,' I linked.

'*I'm working on it*,' he sent back. '*She's not the most cooperative—*'

From where I stood, I could just see the back of Crusher's helmet rising up through the opening in the floor.

'*Never mind*,' I told St. Mathew and broke the connection.

Okay, kid," I said out loud. "Here comes your rematch."

I put everything I had into a forward leap. He turned to shrug me off, but I scrambled around onto his back. The force of my maneuver pitched him on his faceplate. His arms continued to work automatically, swinging the black nunchaku out and around to slam into my back.

I took a hard hit across my shoulders, as he came to his feet. But my arms and legs worked automatically, too. They wrapped themselves around his bulky body and dug in as deeply as possible. I gritted my teeth hard enough to hear them crack and twisted locks off his helmet.

He whorled around violently, scraping me against a rock wall and off his shoulders. His helmet stayed on his head, but he couldn't get it sealed in time.

I stared up at him from the ground as his face expanded to fill the plex and dark, red tissue swelled out of the crack around his neck, where it quickly crystalized in the thin, icy atmosphere. Somehow, he must have been able to still see me, because he brought his chained weapon up above his head, intending to club me in the face—and then he fell forward like a one of the ruined walls of stone, pinning me under him.

The impact knocked my breath out. In a daze, I counted twelve alarms signaling in my suit. Slowly, I worked at getting my wind back.

'*One of these zombies seems to have caught on to what I was doing,*' St. Mathew linked. '*He seems to have jammed the Link I was tapping through Shadow Stone, but I learned that they're not really zombies. They're not really dead, Wolf. So, you should be able to stop your opponent, if you can malf his suit.*'

'*What do I do if he falls on top of me, smartass?*'

The ground trembled.

'*Uh...I sense you need a little help, partner. I've got you located on my suitscam. Want me to come and get you?*'

I didn't like the idea, but responded to it with, '*Yeah. Better you than one of them.*'

A few minutes later, he edged in along the wall and helped lift the weight off my chest.

"Well, well," he radioed. "Turn over a dead body and look what you'll find—the worst private eye on Mars."

I wanted to deck him, but I could barely move. Instead, I sequenced through the suit's alarms and kicked in as many backups as I could find. The ground shook under us again, and St. Mathew almost fell down the stairs.

I leaned forward and looked down at him, asking nonchalantly, "Have you figured out what radio band they're using?"

"Try 880 MHz," he groaned, steadying himself against the wall. "I found it while trying to reach Max."

I turned the dial as we started off together.

A faint transmission started coming in. "...*lassen sie halten!*"

"*Was ist? Was ist? Ich—*"

"*Herr Kommandant spricht—*"

"*Schnell!*"

I linked to St. Mathew. '*What the hell is all that shit?*'

'*German, you ignorant. They're having an argument about whether or not to proceed.*'

'*Proceed with what? It feels like they're shaking the place apart.*'

St. Mathew dropped the Link and gestured for me to follow him.

We crawled out onto a ledge, high up on the eighth level. I linked back to Doc to find out what had happened to our security backup.

'*They're on the way,*' she told me. '*How are you guys doing?*'

'*We've lost Max and I think I killed a zombie.*'

*'What?'*

*'Right now, we're watching Von Roon and his people
fool around with some kind of electronics gizzy down in
the ruins. St. Mathew can tell you more.'*

I came out of the Link and saw that St. Mathew was
still stiff, so Doc must have gotten through to him. Down
below us, a party of more than a dozen people furiously
worked around a network of computer terminals and the
kind of particle wave generators used by icespectors to
see down into the ground. Several members of the group
seemed ready to climb back into their ground cars, while
a tight cluster of people around the Weave Corp CEO
gestured violently in all directions.

I couldn't spot the other two guardian-types that I'd
pegged as Von Roon's "pure-breed zombies." And that
made me real uneasy.

I drew back and lifted my gaze to scan the ruins. If
those two were as tough as Crusher had been—

St. Mathew shook my arm. "Look." He pointed at
the group below us.

The knot of individuals had separated, and I saw
Max standing alone in front of Von Roon. He went to one
of the terminals and began working at it. Von Roon came
over and watched him for a second and then stepped
back. Max spun around and made as if to dash away, but
Von Roon pointed his left hand at him, palm up and
moved his fingers in a rapid series of exercises. For the
first time, I noticed that the hand was almost a half-size

bigger than normal. Max went to his knees and began falling forward, just as a scorching beam of light bit a hole in the ground between St. Mathew and me.

At first I thought it had something to do with what was going on below us, but the trajectory was all wrong. I rolled away from the burnt spot and noted that St. Mathew was moving in the opposite direction. *You'd almost think that we'd rehearsed the maneuver.*

A second beam flashed in the chilled Martian air. The sky was darkening and the canyon began to fill with shadows as evening set in around us.

I huddled behind a low wall, trying to figure out from where the shots had been fired. St. Mathew linked to me, '*I spotted that last one coming from two levels up and to our left.*'

'*That puts you closer to it than me,*' I said.

'*Only by a couple of meters. Are you suggesting I do a little recon?*'

'*I'm suggesting that we haul our butts out of here.*' I broke the link.

We were still in unknown enemy territory with no more effective long-range weapons than rocks. I had a feeling I knew who our attackers were and frankly I wasn't all that interested in making their acquaintance.

Moving cautiously through the darkening ruins, we managed to work our way closer to the top of the gorge. At one point, I could lean over carefully and peer down at the group of workers below. Max still lay face down in the dirt. People stepped over him on their way back and forth between the web of terminals and generators.

I wanted to switch on the spotlight in my helmet, but it would give away our position.

St. Mathew led us up an incline, where we ran directly into our attackers. Like the idiot he was, he rushed at them with enough sudden surprise to knock one of them down and yank his mazer rifle free, just as the other figure turned to fire.

Me? Well, I didn't have much choice in the matter. It was either let the damn fool fry, or jump in with both fists swinging. I cursed St. Mathew's reckless ass and pounded forward, certain that one of us would be dead in the next few seconds. Probably both, since I was getting winded.

A beam from the mazer that St. Mathew was grabbing lanced high into the top of the cliff wall and a brief shower of fist-sized rocks pummeled us.

I drove an elbow into my opponent's side. This guy wasn't half as big as Crusher, but he was quick as hell. I knew right away that I wouldn't get a chance to use my helmet trick on him.

Something heavy and hard hit me in the back, stunning my left arm. Bright mazer fire flew all around me for a second, and I caught a glimpse of St. Mathew and the other guy burning hell out of each other. From where I stooped behind a cracked and ragged wall, there was no sign of the other zombie. I went back to my tactic of rock-throwing and caught my partner's opponent up side of his head with one that pitched him off balance.

St. Mathew took advantage of the moment and tipped him over the edge of the level. Then he radioed that he wanted me to move to where he could lay down cover for us both with his rifle.

I hot footed it over and found he'd taken a couple of minor hits in the forearm and thigh. He's suit was scorched where the Mazer had licked it. I reached out an open hand. "Why don't you let me take charge from here on out?"

It was a reasonable request, I thought, but he flashed me a smile. "What and give up show biz?"

Something deep in his eyes told me this was his superego talking and that we'd need to get out of here fast, or he'd be on permanent stakeout in the Big Nowhere.

I helped him to his feet and tried to take the rifle. He wouldn't give it up, and I seriously considered coldcocking him. The only thing that stopped me was that I knew I'd have to carry him then.

We hobbled into one of the shadowy rooms, just as the piezosand began to faintly glow.

"How do we get out of this maze?" St. Mathew radioed.

"I don't know anymore. Best thing to do is to keep going up until we reach the top of the canyon."

*'Watch out to your left,'* Jonny linked.

And a slim, dark arm made a grab from a dark corner

for St. Mathew's mazer rifle.

I pushed him out of the way and kicked backward into the shadow. True to its name—there was nothing there.

The ground surged underfoot. A portion of the room's roof pounded down next to us.

"Move it, or lose it!" I shouted and rolled out through a sagging archway.

We double-timed up another level and around another corner. I watched our back trail, but the canyon was now almost completely in eclipsing shadow.

'*Okay, kid,*' I linked to Jonny. '*You seem to know what's going on. Where the hell are they?*'

St. Mathew slumped to the ground in obvious pain.

'*They're two levels below you,*' Jonny told me. '*The one called Spirit Lock is badly hurt from his fall, but he's trying to penetrate the Shadow woman's consciousness in order to mentally flow back up the Link to St. Mathew's mind so they can gain control—*'

St. Mathew twisted around suddenly and started firing the mazer in my direction!

I hollered something like, "Son of a shit!" and dove back through a doorway. This was just what I needed—a running battle with my own partner.

'*Thanks for the warning,*' I told Jonny. '*Now how about doing something that will get me out of this!*'

'*Try and stay away from him.*'

'*Wow!*' I said. '*Why didn't I think of that?*' I hustled my butt through a sagging doorway and into another room.

'*Not that way!*' Jonny urged. '*They're coming up after you.*'

'*Well, what then?*'

'*Go left and then down,*' he told me. '*I'm working on something.*'

'*But what'll the zombies do when they meet up with St. Mathew?*'

'*Oh—I see what you mean. They'll kill him.*'

'*Piss in a vacuum! I gotta go back.*'

By now, I was completely unsure of which direction was the right way to go. At least Jonny Jesus could help me navigate the sloops and corridors.

Moments later, in the dull glow of the piezosand, I saw the zombies moving toward me.

'*St. Mathew is still two rooms over, so be careful,*' Jonny said. '*What are you going to do, partner?*'

It was now or never.

I slowed my breathing, hoping it would calm my racing heart. My best shot would be to attack St. Mathew, rather than the other guys. I knew he was running on remote and the zombies were probably having trouble controlling him, due to their wounds and mental efforts. Besides, with him, I'd only have to fight one opponent, instead of two.

And to be perfectly honest, I always liked the idea of knocking his lights out.

I ducked into the room to my left and waited in the

murky darkness with all my helmet lights and instruments turned dark. My play depended on St. Mathew reaching me before Shadow and Spirit did.

I waited.

I waited some more.

*'She's coming at you!'* Jonny warned, just as St. Mathew's wounded body marched through the door. I threw a fist into his stomach, and he bent forward, lighting the room with the brilliant beam of his mazer. I brought a knee up with all the strength I could muster and cracked it solidly into his lowered helmet. He snapped erect, and I kicked him back against the stone wall where he banged his head again, fell to the ground, and didn't move. Damn! Slugging him hadn't been as much fun as I'd figured.

A black hand reached around from behind me and covered my faceplate like a fat spider. I felt my helmet unlocking!

*'It's Shadow,'* Jonny warned, unnecessarily.

I pitched forward and threw the lithe, dark body over my shoulder and against the wall. *'You're a little slow, kid,'* I told Jonny, as I picked up the mazer rifle and fired at where she'd landed. There was nothing there.

*'I told you, I've been busy,'* Jonny answered.

*'How does she do that?'*

*'Here comes Spirit Lock and he's still got the rifle.'*

I gritted my molars. This was where we'd make our stand. I couldn't fight them and carry St. Mathew's unconscious body at the same time. I'd have to shoot it out with one of them, while the other one snuck up on us out of the shadows, or Tripleye would have to hire itself two new ops.

A short beam blazed in through the doorway from around a corner. *'She's on your right!'* Jonny cried.

I fired where he told me, but saw nothing.

Another beam sliced through the rocks, burning within millimeters of my left shoulder. Out of the corner of my eye, I saw St. Mathew's arm move.

*'She's behind you.'*

I spun around and fired again. The room flashed white for a second, and I thought I saw her slipping out the rear door. Another beam lit the room. I turned back and let loose a series of bursts that clawed holes in the wall where Spirit hid.

St. Mathew's body started to get up.

I rushed over and kicked at his helmet. His hands came up and caught my foot, twisting it, throwing me off balance. "What the hell's the matter with you?" he radioed.

*'His temporary Link has faded,'* Jonny said. *'They can't get to him anymore.'*

*'Can they get to me?'*

*'I'm covering for you, partner. But she's on your right and moving fast!'*

I spun around and hit something solidly with the butt of my rifle. I saw her fall back into St. Mathew's arms, and then she was gone.

"I hate to sound redundant," I radioed to him, "But let's get the hell out here!"

Another fierce beam shot across my faceplate, dazzling my vision. A hand clutched at my left forearm, and I tried to pull away.

"It's me," St. Mathew said. "Come on!"

We hurried out the rear door not knowing what to expect next. My vision started to clear as we made our way up an incline to the next level.

'*Go right*,' Jonny told me, and I pulled St. Mathew in that direction. We were now almost directly above the area where Spirit had been hiding. I looked over the edge and saw something moving below.

"What next?" St. Mathew asked.

I lined the sights of the rifle and said, "I'm going to kill me another zombie."

A dark hand came out of nowhere and yanked the rifle to one side. I cursed as my beam went wide of its mark and three other beams shot up from various directions below us.

"They're bringing in reinforcements," St. Mathew said. "That's wonderful!"

I hunkered down next to him behind a wall. "What's so fucking wonderful about being surrounded?"

He smiled weakly behind his scarred faceplate. "We can attack in any direction.

I shook my head and looked down at my mazer rifle.

"Not with this thing. We're almost out of firepower."

"Shit!" he said.

"Watch your mouth," I told him as we began to crawl through an archway.

I called to Jonny. *'Where do we go next?'*

*'I've been talking to the Snot.'*

*'You've been* what?'

*'It's a lot closer to me than you might think.'*

*'Look, kid,'* I said. *'At this point, I don't know what to think. Just get us out of here.'*

*'She's behind you, again!'*

I swung the rifle around like a bludgeon, while yelling, "Duck," and connected with something solid in the darkness.

"Watch it, Wolf," St. Mathew warned. "You almost hit me."

"Just keep away from me," I said as we moved through another room. "And for god's sake, duck when I tell you."

The ground shrugged violently and the path we were following dropped away from beneath our feet. I fell flat, rolling and tumbling down a level, almost losing the rifle in the process. All around me stones were bouncing and walls were crumbling into piles of rocky debris. The piezosand lit the night like rocket exhaust from the intense vibration and then quickly began to dim.

St. Mathew was hanging halfway over the edge of a deep drop, struggling with a pool of blackness.

I came to my feet, rushed over and kicked into the darkness above him, sending it sailing silently over the side.

He got up and looked over the edge. "How can she do that? I know she's a master of disguise, but—"

"What the hell are you talking about?"

There was a strange look in his eyes. "I think I'm in love," he said.

The ground moved again, and I cursed Von Roon for whatever he was doing to cause a huge stone to peel itself from the canyon wall and chop through six levels on its way past where we stood.

'*Go back and turn left,*' Jonny told me.

We didn't have any choice in the matter. It was either that or a long drop down. I was checking the rifle to make sure it still functioned, when St. Mathew shoved me against a pile of rubble. I didn't even have the energy to complain.

'*A little farther,*' Jonny said. '*Hurry.*'

A beam sliced above our heads.

'*Shit, kid. We're heading right into them!*'

'*You've got to. It's the only way out.*'

Why didn't that surprise me? Two more beams flashed at us from a huddle of figures not twenty meters in front of our noses.

'*No,*' Jonny said. '*Fire at the wall next to you.*'

Another beam flashed past me. Something dark was on St. Mathew again.

The ground shook and seemed to tilt. More beams hurtled at us. They were coming closer.

'*Now!*' Jonny told me, as I fell to one knee from a jolting tremor.

This felt like the real thing—a full-scale marsquake that threatened to swallow us whole and grind us to a pulpy ooze. Massive chunks of rock poured down, as I squeezed the trigger and burned a hole in the wall. Something hit me from behind. A rock? A beam? A body? I don't know, but I had a terrifying image of being buried alive.

The quake picked me up and threw me ass over elbows through the wall I'd just blasted. St. Mathew tried to radio to me, but all I heard was a stream of grunts and vowels. Some of them were mine.

Smoke filled the passageway. No, it wasn't smoke. It was a fog of dust particles hanging in the light gravity. My helmet was alive with alarm signals. My lower legs were buried in a heavy wash of rubble and silt.

Three meters to my right, the glove of a St. Mathew's pressuresuit jutted up out of the rocky slag like a clawed headstone. I hoped there was a hand in it.

Dampening the alarms in my suit and drawing myself free from a mound of shattered stone, I dropped down on my knees and began digging around the hand. "Saint Mat," I radioed. "Jules. Let me hear from you."

After a couple of extended minutes, I found the backside of his helmet. He was lying on his side buried beneath the residue of the quake/explosion. I looked around for something to help pry him out, but there was nothing in the tunnel but dirt. The opening that I'd blasted was completely sealed with a jumble of boulders and sand.

I kept digging, until I could get around to an angle that fully exposed his faceplate. He looked up and blew me a kiss.

"You shithead," I yelped. "This isn't some game we're playing. Get out of there."

He radioed back, "Help me up, shamus. I've got a big rock on my back."

"You've got one in your head, too. Is that shadow woman still within you?"

"Who can tell?" he said, pushing stones away from his hips. "Especially in all this mess."

I began trying to get my bearing through the haze of rock dust. The spotlight on my helmet didn't work, but the vibration from the quakes had stimulated the piezos- and causing the walls and ceiling to glow richly. I thought I saw a long tunnel stretching out before us.

I tried linking to Doc Pat. *'We're in some sort of empty passageway. Jonny led us here. I don't think we'll need that security backup, but a rescue team would be kinda nice.'*

The ground vibrated again beneath my feet.

Doc linked back. *'The security team never made it to the Xanth Plains. A fissure opened up and their ground-*

*cars fell in. We're taking a lot of pounding here. The aftershock might—Oh, god!'*

*'What happened?'*

*'The building's starting to buckle. I've got to get out! Our files—'*

The ground shook again. *'Forget the files and get your ass out of there, Doc, right now!'*

I got no response and that really worried me.

*'Follow the tunnel,'* Jonny said. *'It'll take you back to the ruins in Achilles City.'*

*'I suppose you got that info through the Snot,'* I said.

*'Just hurry.'*

We stumbled down the tunnel. I lied to St. Mathew, telling him that I'd contacted Doc on the Link and that she'd instructed us to take this "secret passageway."

"They must have been seismologically prospecting for the treasure and hit a fault line," he told me.

I realized that this was the first time in days that we'd been able to compare notes. "What treasure? I thought they were after control of the Snot."

He stopped limping. "Say, what is that stuff anyway?"

"A lab tech at Blue Star Industries calls it a plasmoid, or something. Says it's intelligent and might even be what's left of the original Martians. You'd know some of this, if you followed standard investigative procedure, instead of running of like a lone—"

"Wolf?" he said.

"What?"

"I was just finishing your sentence for you."

"I can finish my own sentence, all right?"

We walked over and around more rubble. Any second, the tunnel could slam shut or crash down on us. I hoped the trip back wouldn't take as long as my drive out to rescue St. Mathew. My suit couldn't hold out much longer.

"I just thought I'd check on things to be sure there wasn't any hazard, before any of you guys got here," he said lamely. It was the closest thing to an apology I'd ever heard him say. He shrugged. "Everybody's been having so many troubles lately."

This didn't sound like the Jules St. Mathew I knew and hated. "It's nice to see that you're getting introspective at your age. My old man used to say that deep reflective thought is a hallmark of a quality private eye."

I thought that might get me a laugh, but all he said was: "I'm truly tempted to confess everything to you, Wolf, but—"

"What's this now? Is the great St. Mathew willing to admit a mistake?"

He shut up. We continued easing along the empty corridor.

Once again, the ground shook. I hoped it was from the settling effects of an aftershock and suddenly pictured all of Achilles City crumbled into ruins. It looked like Von Roon had gotten what he'd wanted.

'*Hey, kid,*' I said to Jonny. '*I'm running low on ox. How much longer before we get out of here?*'

'*Up ahead you'll find a hole that has broken open that leads into the ancient part of the city. Keep your suits on. There's been a lot of damage and some of the atmosphere has leaked away.*'

I passed the word to St. Mathew, and we tried to double-time it until we spotted the crack in the wall and ceiling. From there, we at last came out into the old Achilles Ruins, and that was an apt phrase for what we found.

Holy chaos, everywhere, in dim light. Some of the areas and structures had turned completely to rubble, others were seemingly untouched. The storage center with its passageway we'd used to escape, fortunately, was the least affected by the force of the quake. Maybe the old Achillians knew more about their planet's geology than we did. They had built what now appeared to be an annex to their main city in a cavern which we only used for the storage of essential materials, like water and high-protein staples.

Fumes had leeched from the power centers where we combined electrolyzed hydrogen with surface carbon di-ox to produce methane. Electrolysis was how we got a lot of our oxygen, too. While the air around St. Mathew and I still registered high in methane, it was barely breathable, so we risked removing our helmets.

More signs of the disaster came into view as we

moved on. I saw two evacuated storage vehicles—one teetering precariously on the edge of a gaping fissure that had split the roadway and the other had been flattened by a pile of fallen debris.

The gravity compensators had gone haywire. Whole structures had started tumbling down while under standard conditions. Then, when the systems failed and the normal, lower gravity had taken hold, people began tossing boulders around in order to free the crushed or trapped disaster victims.

A few frightened survivors crawled timidly into their collapsed apartments to save the damnedest things. A holo, an appliance, a coloring book. I was grateful that I had most of my mods with me, especially my favorites containing the jazzblues. I began to understand what the people around me were trying to do: maintain identity.

A lot of rescuers worked with their bare hands to free the trapped from structures that were cracked, crumbling and badly sagging. We helped where we could and avoided buckling corridors. The bodies and blood reminded me of war.

Dust was everywhere. It layered everything and everyone. I heard cries, and tappings and moanings coming from beneath shattered buildings and from behind collapsed passages choked with huge chunks of still-crumbling dirt.

An ancient crack in the ground beneath the Main Mall had given way, allowing several buildings to drop as much as three meters. Dozens of visitors had been crushed to death when massive panels had broken off and cascaded down from the sides of the cavern walls.

Some buildings had collapsed in a heap. A wide crevasse had opened beneath the Gov Admin Center, tearing it in half as one wing dropped two meters into the depression.

The piezosand still gave light and the ground itself generated heat from the stress, but electrical lines were a lurking danger. The greatest fear was fire. It could consume us all in a day and eat up our oxygen. Tanks of pressurized carbon diox foam would help prevent it, but these would have to be used sparingly to avoid contaminating what was left of our atmosphere.

I saw it all with dead eyes. The yawning chasms. The ripped apart, splintered duralloy. The twisted tangle of power and Vax lines. Apartments were at all angles, everything topsy-turvy and spilled into the hot, dust-choked corridors. People carrying survivors on make-shift litters. One man with his wife thrown across his back, blundered into a med station, apparently unaware that she was already dead.

St. Mathew and I finally reached what was left of the Tripleye offices. The pavement had burst open around it. Two survivors were dragging away a body that had been pinned by the leg inside the collapsed building. There had been no hesitation. No arguing. They had administered a local anesthetic and sawed off the leg below the knee, in order to save the body. The body was Doc Pat's and she seemed not only grateful to be alive, but genuinely relieved to see that I had rescued my partner.

I think that's when I knew I'd follow her through hell and back. In a very real way, I just had…

⁏ᎧᎩ

There was little sense in continuing the report. Wolf slipped out of report mode and shut off the new Ultra-Vax and walked to the opening in his tent to watch as the remaining citizens of Achilles City continued with the dig out efforts. He let his mind drift.

Many people had moved up to live among the wilting plants under the domes near the transport stations. Others, like Wolf, had pitched pressure tents where they could find clear space in the tunnels. It wasn't the first time the city had faced disaster.

You didn't place a civilization under the ground without being prepared for occasional cave-ins. *That's exactly how my old man died back in 2090*, Wolf thought. Rescuing someone he hardly knew from a collapsed tunnel.

He checked the time, noting he was late for the survivors gathering, and walked outside to meet a couple of workmen who were clearing out the rubble from across the corridor.

One of them was finishing a conversation with the

comment, "…both parents are dead, but the baby's un-hurt."

Death had been the main topic of discussion in Achilles for the last few days. Almost three thousand people had been killed in the severe aftershock that had rippled through a fault in the Martian surface. Another seven thousand were seriously injured. And just about everybody had lost something in the quake: a home, a friend, or a relative. In the midst of all the devastation and dig out, Von Roon and what was left of his crew had gotten off planet in a private shuttle.

Wolf stuck a battered fedora on his bald head and picked his way toward the center of town. The heavy grav equipment had been released from essential service around the geo-therm stations. The units were beginning to churn and shovel and shove the rubble from the middle of the corridors. The homeless, lost, and weary were queuing up for food and water from the relief stations at major intersections. A network of portable Vax comput-ers had been set up there too, so that messages from miss-ing friends and relatives could be posted.

According to a major announcement, an official cen-sus was to be taken that afternoon in the Main Mall in front of what was left of the Gov Admin Center. Wolf stepped over rubble and debris to join his fellow citizens at the site.

*Will we give up?*

The question seemed to be on everyone's mind. *Why*

*re-build Achilles City on top of what was obviously a prime fault line? Why live here at all?*

Someone from the gov was giving a speech to the several thousand survivors. Wolf looked up and realized that he knew the man. It was Arthur McBain, the agency's gov liaison. He had never thought much of the elderly, frail man, but he listened now as McBain's words rang across the crowded Mall.

"…only people who don't know what they're talking about, people who've never been here and seen our fair city. They are the only ones questioning the future of Achilles." Arthur stood at the top of a broken stairway, sleeves rolled back and head held high. It seemed to Wolf that the man's voice held a quality of calm certitude. "This ground is hallowed now with the blood of many of our finest citizens. Their sad remains will now go back into eco-bank, so that you can go on. As your new governor, I pray that you look around at these ruins and the people next to you with pride and hope in your heart. These are the best ruins and the damned finest people in the entire system!"

A mild cheer rolled up from the crowd.

"Supplies and relief are pouring in from all points, with the purpose of helping us to keep this city alive. And I fully intend to keep fighting."

Jonny spoke in his mind. *'I told Chico what happened, just as you asked. She wishes you well, but she's not coming back.'*

Wolf sighed. *'When's the baby due?'* he asked Jon-ny.

*'Another couple of months. He's fine, too.'*

Another cheer rose from the crowd and Wolf went back to listening to McBain.

"A day will soon come," the elderly man said, "when we will put this rubble behind us and rise up a stronger, more focused, a more capable people than ever before, to take our place beside the major system corps and show them that Achilles is a community to be relied upon and reckoned with."

Wolf spotted Doc Pat and St. Mathew at the back of the crowd. He eased his way over to stand with them. There was a white bandage around the dark skin below the woman's right knee. She would have to function from now on with a prosthetic leg.

"How you feeling?" he asked his boss.

"Don't worry about me," the black woman said. "In a way, I sort of deserve this little loss."

Wolf looked questioningly at St. Mathew, who shrugged. "She claims that she messed up much too often in not believing Jannings's story, or not suspecting Chico of passing info to Von Roon—"

"—and not taking the Link until it was almost too late," Doc Pat said. "Believe me, this injury is a gift. One I intend, as soon as possible, to return."

Wolf was mildly surprised by this confession. "Sort of an Achilles Heel, huh?"

"That's a very bad joke, Baldy," St. Mathew said, "considering the current state of the city.

"Oh, I don't know," Wolf answered. "Take a look around."

The survivors had begun to celebrate the dawn of a new era. McBain's words had somehow caught hold and people were beginning to act like the fortunate few who had come through a crisis unharmed. There was free-flowing drink and food arriving from well-wishers and the entire census day was turning into a happy one.

Doc Pat smiled. "I see what you mean, Wolf. Looks like everything will be replitropic."

"Listen," St. Mathew said. "I've got to get Doc here back to the hospital. She's helping treat stress-fatigued patients. Want to come and empty bed pans?"

Despite the implied insult, Wolf laughed. "I'm supposed to be on second trick dig-out down in Dirtown." He rubbed his bare pate. "Besides, I need a shave."

"We've got to get together soon to re-build the agency," Doc advised. "There's a lot of unfinished business."

"And some big debts to be paid," St. Mathew added. "None of these people here know how Von Roon initiated the quake."

"We'll get him," Wolf said, mirroring McBain's calm certitude.

"How about this Friday at my place?" St. Mathew said.

"Your place? It would be a pleasure." Wolf stared at

Doc and then back at Jules. "Ever since you joined the team, we've been wondering where you live."

"Well, you're in for a surprise. Meet us at the hospital and I'll take you there."

The crowd was beginning to disperse. Wolf waved to his two friends and thought again of Chico and the baby.

*'How 'bout a little jazz, partner?'* Jonny asked as Wolf trudged off to join the work gang at the mines.

*'Good idea, kid,'* he answered, slipping a mod into the top of his head. *'Ever hear Michael Nasmith's "Rio"?'*

*'Does it have a beat I can dance to?'*

*'Not in my head.'*

THE END

The agents of Tripleye will return in a few months.

Continue reading for a preview of

# OXYMORON

By John Hegenberger

# CHAPTER 1

*YONDER*

Eric Von Roon felt the distant, faint trembling in the Link. He hovered his thumb over the detonator that would destroy the ship.

⁂

The Vax went *Breep* and spat its printout onto the deck, just as the ops of Tripleye came aboard. Jules St. Mathew picked it up and glanced at its contents. "It's for you," he said, handing the message to Doc Pat.

The black woman accepted it from her wheelchair. "I told Mishko we'd be meeting here and to forward any important updates concerning Jonny and the Link." Pat read the message. "She says she's sorry to hear about the quake and is glad we all made it through in one piece. I—I didn't tell her about my leg."

The third op, Dan "Wolf" Archerson, had been wandering around the ship's cabin, bending to inspect various items and instruments in St. Mathew's vessel.

It was a gaudy ship by anyone's standards. Jules was known to be ego-centric, but having mirrors installed over the pilot's seat was a bit presumptuous, and Wolf said so.

"It…ah…makes the cabin seem bigger than it really is," Jules explained.

"And you've got a mean collection of music discs," Wolf continued. "I might want to copy some of these for my mods."

Jules turned his attention back to Doc Pat. "What's Chico say about Von Roon?"

"Holy shit!" Wolf exclaimed from behind them. "You've got an original Gershwin here."

Pat and Jules exchanged glances.

"Uh…say, Wolf," Jules called. "We're trying to get a strategy session going here, remember?"

The bald op walked forward to confront the ship's owner. "Listen, Mr. Ego, nobody wants to get that malf Von Roon more than me. So knock off the impromptu lectures, okay? Where'd you get this ship, anyway? Salvage from one of your 'secret adventures'? Must cost a mint to launch it."

"I won her in a VisionDuel, three years ago from a hot-shot economist from Earth."

"You licensed to pilot this thing?"

"It took a while, but, yeah, I can fly it." Jules stroked the control board, lovingly. "The previous owner called her the *Busted Flush*, whatever that means, but I changed her name to *Yonder*, as in cold, black, and dangerous."

"Sounds like you're talking about Doc Pat."

Upon hearing her name, Patricia Emory looked up, worry lining her forehead.

Her mind continued to sort through the info she'd just read, while her two employee's bickered and traded barbs. If what Mishko said were true, and Von Roon had met Chico at the Triage labs on Ceres during the Belt War, then he must, therefore, also know about the Link.

Pat tried to fit this into place with what she already knew from their recent encounters with the head of Weave Corp and his Neo-socialist bodyguards. But the pain in her right leg continued to throb, keeping her from thinking clearly.

"Hey, you two," she called, just as Wolf and Jules were settling into another of their impromptu arguments, "I need your help on this."

Jules smiled into Wolf's face. "Saved again by the boss, baldy."

# About the Author

John Hegenberger writes adventure, mystery, science, and horror fiction. Born and raised in the heart of the heartland, Columbus, Ohio, he is the author of *Tripleye* series and the *Stan Wade LA PI* series from Black Opal Books. Father of three, a tennis enthusiast, collector of silent films and OTR, hiker, Francophile, B.A. Comparative Literature, ex-navy, ex-comic book dealer, ex-marketing exec at Exxon, AT&T, and IBM, he has been happily married for 47 years and counting.

Over the years, he's published fifteen books of mystery, science fiction, and western adventures...but mostly comedy. Follow him at johnhegenberger.com and have fun.